What the c [barcode: D1467171]

"I had a hard time put____ down when I started reading it... it was an outsta____ _stallment to a fantastic series." ~ *Julia, Romance Junkies*

"Ms. Walker has done it again...a wonderfully creative author. She is able to create characters that capture and endear themselves to her fans." ~ *Dianne Nogueras, Ecataromance Golden Angel Review at Fallen Angel Reviews*

"I am continuously spellbound by the writings of Shiloh Walker...created a dynamic gripping plot that left me breathless..." ~ *Contessa, Fallen Angel Reviews*

SHILOH WALKER

BEN
and
Shadoe
THE HUNTERS

ELLORA'S CAVE
ROMANTICA PUBLISHING

An Ellora's Cave Romantica Publication

www.ellorascave.com

Ben and Shadoe

ISBN #1419952420
ALL RIGHTS RESERVED.
Ben and Shadoe Copyright© 2005 Shiloh Walker
Edited by: Pamela Campbell
Cover art by: Syneca

Electronic book Publication: January, 2005
Trade paperback Publication: July, 2005

With the exception of quotes used in reviews, this book may not be reproduced or used in whole or in part by any means existing without written permission from the publisher, Ellora's Cave Publishing, Inc.® 1056 Home Avenue, Akron OH 44310-3502.

This book is a work of fiction and any resemblance to persons, living or dead, or places, events or locales is purely coincidental. The characters are productions of the authors' imagination and used fictitiously.

Warning:

The following material contains graphic sexual content meant for mature readers. *Ben and Shadoe* has been rated *E-rotic* by a minimum of three independent reviewers.

Ellora's Cave Publishing offers three levels of Romantica™ reading entertainment: S (S-ensuous), E (E-rotic), and X (X-treme).

S-*ensuous* love scenes are explicit and leave nothing to the imagination.

E-*rotic* love scenes are explicit, leave nothing to the imagination, and are high in volume per the overall word count. In addition, some E-rated titles might contain fantasy material that some readers find objectionable, such as bondage, submission, same sex encounters, forced seductions, etc. E-rated titles are the most graphic titles we carry; it is common, for instance, for an author to use words such as "fucking", "cock", "pussy", etc., within their work of literature.

X-*treme* titles differ from E-rated titles only in plot premise and storyline execution. Unlike E-rated titles, stories designated with the letter X tend to contain controversial subject matter not for the faint of heart.

Also by Shiloh Walker:

Ben and Shadoe
The Hunters

Dedication

This one…obviously…is for Lora.

Thanks for being such a sweet lady!

Thanks to Pam <hug>

And always…love to my family…you are everything to me.

Prologue

Marcus could see her leaving the dorm, smell her. Something about her seemed oddly familiar. She smiled shyly at the golden-haired boy walking next to her, ducking her head, scooping her hair out of her face, acting coy — an act. Just an act.

He had come to see the boy, his newest recruit; a werewolf one of his werewolf underlings had bitten and changed. And this one showed such promise. But Marcus lost all interest in Jimmy as he stared at the young woman.

Her scent... Damn it, why was it so familiar?

Sweet, hot, potent...

Potent.

Then he knew.

Inherents smelled something like that. She smelled like a wolf. Like a shifter, almost.

And like magick. Almost.

But she didn't move like a wolf. Didn't act like one.

And she didn't have the feel of a witch about her.

She was a puzzle.

And he would just have to solve her.

Jimmy Duncan stared at the ground as Marcus paced around him. The fear the older, more powerful wolf could induce disgusted him almost as much as it called to him. He wanted that same control over others. Too bad he didn't realize it was a power the average werewolf just couldn't have.

"I saw your little girlfriend," Marcus murmured as he flopped onto the couch.

"Jillian?" Jimmy asked, lifting his eyes slowly. "She's not exactly—"

"I don't care what she is. I want her."

"But—"

A low, dangerous growl rumbled out of Marcus' throat and Jimmy immediately dropped his eyes. He knew what happened to those who questioned the dominant wolf. He had seen it, right after he had been changed. He knew, all right. And while it had amused the hell out of him to watch it, he had no intention of seeing it done to him.

"I understand," Jimmy said slowly, bitterly. He had looked forward to feeling that hot little pussy. Probably virgin. Definitely an innocent—he could tell, just by her scent. He could smell her uncertainty, her fear, her young lust. It was amazing, the things he could read now.

Marcus smiled. "Good. And maybe I can even be generous enough to share," he responded.

Jimmy nodded, and forced a smile. After all, seconds was better than nothing.

Marcus watched, with a smile on his face, as she followed Jimmy into the house. His pale gray eyes glittered as he shifted against the railing upstairs, resting his chin on his fist, listening to her soft murmur. Her voice was as clear as day.

"Such a pretty house, Jimmy. It's so big," she mused, amazed. She had big eyes. Soft skin. The pulse in her neck called to him like a siren's song.

As Jimmy stood aside to let her pass, he slid a look upstairs and caught the older wolf's eyes. And smiled.

The entire left side of her face burned as if it were on fire. Her lower lip throbbed, oozing blood that trickled down her chin and neck to stain the silk blouse she'd been so proud of. Now, her only conscious thought was to burn it, if she made it out of this damn house alive.

Her own rapid breathing sounded impossibly loud as she made her way down the back steps, listening for any sound that they might have found her. From somewhere inside the house, she heard Jimmy bellow out her name as she took the last step and rounded the corner into the kitchen. And freedom, just a few feet away, if she could only make it to the back door in time.

Time's up.

His heavy footsteps sounded down the hall, heading her way. She flew through the room, hands closing around the doorknob just as he entered the kitchen.

"Stupid bitch," he panted, wiping the blood away from his mouth with the back of his hand as he came for her.

Jerking frantically on the doorknob, she sobbed in frustration as it refused to open.

When it finally opened, she tore through it with a relieved sob, moving fast, too fast. But it wasn't Jimmy she had to worry about. The other man was there. Waiting for her. His eyes... *Oh, God*, she prayed, desperately. *Help me.* His eyes were glowing.

Backing away from him, she edged her way around him. But Jimmy was at her back and he grabbed her arms and laughed, his voice deeper, rougher, and so amused. He loved every second of her fear. She could feel his pleasure, sense it somehow.

Jillian struggled and smashed her head back into his, the back of her head crashing into his nose — she heard it crunch, felt blood start to pour down her neck as he screamed. The blood smelled hot, coppery and salty.

"Stupid bitch!" he screamed in a garbled voice. "You broke my nose!"

"One soft, practically human female doing such damage?" the other man asked, laughing as Jimmy shoved her away. "She's not even one of us, really. She has the scent, but just barely. She's more mortal than wolf. How can you let her hurt you?"

"She's a strong little bitch, go see for yourself."

He was so strong — Jillian thought, catching herself just in time to keep from falling. Both men looked surprised that she

11

was still on her feet and she lunged around Jimmy's kneeling body, back into the house, slamming the door behind her and locking it.

A weapon.

A fist came crashing through the door. *How in the hell?* It was solid wood. She yelped, then bit back the sound before it could turn into a scream as a hand came through the hole in the door and unlocked it. The door swung open and the other man stood there, watching her.

He stepped toward her, laughing softly. She plunged her hand into the sink and her fingers closed around the smooth wooden hilt of a kitchen knife. A heavy one. Whipping it out, she sidestepped the stranger and thrust it in front of her. "Get away from me," she whispered through clenched teeth.

Jimmy moved into the room, blood and mucus streaming down his face as he glared at her with angry, evil eyes that gleamed in the harsh kitchen light. *Why did they look red?*

"Take the knife away, pup," the stranger said softly, leaning against the counter and folding his arms. "I'd like to see her naked."

"Come near me and I'll gut you," she warned.

"Bad, stupid little bitch," Jimmy said, ignoring her. Wagging a finger at her, he said, "I'm gonna hurt you now."

She jabbed at him, and cried out when he hit the side of her wrist, shooting a jolt of pain up her arm, knocking her weapon away. Then he lunged for her, taking her down to the cold tile floor, grinding his pelvis against her.

"Go ahead and cry," he whispered as he leaned down and bit her neck. Wrenching both hands over her head, he said, "It only makes it better for us. We love fear."

Whimpering, she turned her face away as he used his free hand to rip aside her bloodstained blouse. "Too damn little of you," he muttered. "But you got enough fight to make this fun."

Humiliated, frightened, and angry, she jerked again on her hands, sweat making them slippery enough to almost slide away. At the same time, she brought her knee up as he was shifting to straddle her thighs. His howl of pain echoed in her ears as she scrambled away from him, sliding on her butt as she clambered to gain her feet. One hand locked around her ankle and he brought her back.

"I'm not gonna hurt you now," he rasped. White-faced, pupils dilated, he hissed, "I'm gonna kill you."

His face...oh, hell, his face... The bones were lengthening, stretching, the skin pulling tight over it, darkening, and his teeth as he struck—not at her neck, but at the fleshy mound of her right breast—the white-hot pain ripped through her as he tore the flesh...

And then he was gone, flying through the air and crashing into a wall.

"Pup, she is mine, not yours," a cool, collected voice said.

The other man was taking his place, his eyes hot and burning, hungry. Some deeply buried instinct whispered, *Run. You have to run...the smell of blood...the fight has stirred his lust.*

One hand reached out, striking him in the face, his neck, anything to keep her from being pinned again. Her other hand frantically searched the floor as he jerked her skirt up. As he ripped her panties away, her fingers closed once more around the smooth wooden hilt.

"No," she whispered when he reached down to free himself from his well-pressed khakis. He never paid any attention to her hands, not the one shoving at his face, and not the one holding the knife that she shoved into his ribs, parting the flesh like butter.

Scalding waves of blood poured over her as she took the knife out and struck home a second, and then a third time. By then, blood was bubbling out from his lips as he stared down at her with wide, shocked eyes. Angry eyes, as he whispered, "You're going to regret that, little wolf."

With a strength born of panic, she pushed him away and cowered against the counter as he shoved to his feet and staggered to the wall, pressing his hands against his numerous wounds, wheezing gasps of air filling the room. "Jimmy... Make her pay," he rasped, staring at her with a nasty light in his eyes.

Jimmy lunged at her and took her down. Jillian fell, screaming, feeling her head strike the floor. She clutched the knife and drove it upwards as hard as she could, twisting, shoving it higher and higher, feeling bile rise in her throat as her *hand* entered his body... *His heart, if you don't destroy it, he won't die.* Something was burning in her hand, something hot, like fire and as she screamed, it exploded outward from her hand.

A gray puff of smoke drifted out of Jimmy's mouth, then a froth of blood. His eyes went dim, that angry, swirling, glowing light gone. And he fell lifeless on top of her.

She turned her head just in time to see the other man fall to his knees and groan as a wolf seemed to leap out of his skin. And then she passed out.

Chapter One

Jillian awoke with the scream trapped in her throat, sweat covering her body. For a moment, she thought it was the blood that had flowed out of Jimmy's body after she had damn near gutted him.

The light from the corridor poured in through the tiny window of her cell door.

Her eyes instinctively sought the clock on the wall, marking away the time as she had for the past six years. After midnight. The anniversary, she thought with a ragged laugh as she sat up, dangling her skinny legs over the side of her cot. Her feet rested on the cold floor.

Six years to the day since she had killed Jimmy Duncan, a man guilty of raping more than seven young women in the tiny rural town of Buxley, in southern Mississippi. That particular fact had not come out until his picture had been flashed in so many papers that one, then another, and another of those girls had slowly stepped out of hiding. Coming forward only because their attacker was dead, and couldn't make good on his threat to kill them.

A man who was the grandson of a state Senator, the only son of the town mayor, and the heir to the Duncan millions.

The second man she had described, the other blood found at the scene of the vicious attack that the prosecutor had painted around her as he had tried to set her up for the death penalty— well, that body had never been found.

Because the body had run away in the form of a wolf. *Werewolf...*

You're going to regret that, little wolf. His deep, gruff voice rose out of her memories to torment her. *Little wolf? What had he meant? How had she killed Jimmy?*

If the state cop who had found her hadn't been relatively new to the area, and unaware of the hold the Duncans had on southern Mississippi, she probably would have been serving out a life sentence, or sitting on death row. But Beth Starkey hadn't been aware that the dead man on the floor was the local golden boy. And if she had been aware, it was unlikely she would have cared. All she had seen was the battered, beaten little thing who lay unconscious on the floor, her clothes ripped off her body, bruises forming everywhere, blood all over her, a bloody, sooty, pulpy mass in one hand that tested to be Jimmy's heart. Another pile of bloody clothes lay off to the side, but no body was ever found for them.

If it had been any other of the state cops, or any of the locals, the scene wouldn't have been meticulously recorded. She wouldn't have been hand-delivered to a sympathetic young resident who didn't give a damn about the Duncan dynasty.

Instead, thanks to a cop with an unbendable code of honor and a medical resident with kind eyes, she was being released in three days, after serving five years for manslaughter.

Of course, if it had been anybody other than a Duncan, she would never have served any time. Though she only recalled bits and pieces of the final minutes right before Jimmy Duncan died, she knew he had tried to rape her, knew there had been another man in the house who had been a willing participant in the game. The judge and jury had known it—she had seen it in their eyes.

With a scowl of disgust, she forced the self-pity aside. Jillian had no time to feel sorry for herself. Easing her body up from the cot, she rolled her neck and shoulders and went to the small desk with a stack of books.

Three days. Three days, and she was free.

Free? That thought made her pause.

Free to do what? Live out the rest of her life as a convicted felon. So what that she had earned her college degree? Who cared that she was fast on her way to becoming one of the bestselling horror writers in the country, thanks to her own nightmares about Jimmy and the unknown stranger?

She flipped open a book on local ghosts and sighed. *Get to work, Jillian. Just get to work.*

* * * * *

Jillian Morgan.

No. Her real name is Shadoe. Shadoe Wallace.

"Jillian," he told himself. She had been Jillian for more than twenty years. He didn't expect his appearance in her life to change that. Hell, she probably didn't want anything to do with her heritage, not after what people such as he had done.

His dark golden-brown eyes locked on the woman who walked slowly down the street, looking around as if unsure of what to do with herself. She had her arms wrapped nervously around her body, and she jumped at every little sound.

And her heartbeat… He could hear it as it jumped and quickened every time somebody walked too close.

So full of fear.

If she had consented to see him five years ago, they could have started to work on that. He had been trying to talk to her from the beginning but she had never once allowed it.

But now, she was on the outside. And she couldn't run far enough. Her soft brown hair blew gently around her sweet, heart-shaped face as she slowed to a stop in front of a bookstore, smiling absently. He could see what she was staring at, even though she was a good hundred feet away.

A display of Lorelei Dubois books. *Have No Mercy.* He knew who she was, knew exactly how long she had been writing for the small electronic press that had moved into paperbacks only a year earlier.

Benjamin had no doubt where the nightmares behind the books came from. If he had gotten to Marcus just a little sooner—

His breath slowed as she stretched, almost absently, like a lazy little cat. The motion thrust her pert, rounded breasts against the cotton of her shirt, the crowns of her nipples peaking against it, and Ben's throat went dry. She started back down the street and his eyes focused on the tight little ass in her jeans as his body went on red alert. Her scent drifted to him on the wind, warm, ripe female and his cock started to throb.

Damn it.

This could be a problem.

He was here to protect her, to warn her, to teach her. And considering she had been living with her head in the sand for more than twenty years, that wasn't going to be an easy task. Being attracted to her was going to make it even more difficult— but if he felt the wolf inside him, felt the call of hers...

There was no if.

She was an Inherent born, if not yet changed. And he was a very gifted Inherent, a Hunter to the Council, and one of the few who had a touch of witchery through his mother's side of the family. He was a powerful witch, and that was how he had found her, but he suspected what he had in his veins was nothing compared to what lay untapped inside the woman in front of him.

Jillian had more than a touch.

Her mother had gifted her with such powerful witchcraft that it was amazing the earth didn't tremble as she walked. That a powerful, evil, dark seeker hadn't found her and tried to subjugate her.

Amazing that he had found her first, and was thinking that their powers and magicks wouldn't call to the other?

There was no if.

Stop it, Ben. We don't even know if she has the abilities, he told himself, shaking his head. He could smell something other than human on her, but that didn't mean she was an Inherent like her father had been. And the magick he smelled on her didn't mean she was a witch like her mother had been. She had gone more than a decade past the time when she should have first shifted. And no witch could ignore the call of magick for more than twenty years. Just because some old witch saw her thirty years ago, years before her birth, and said she would come in time to help fight some unknown war...

Visions were always subject to change. And maybe it was another Inherent.

Hell, if she was a witch, an Inherent, she would have changed when that werewolf attacked her years ago. If she had...and if she had still been sentenced to jail...

And damn it, it had been Agnes Milcher who'd had the vision. Agnes...

Even as solitary as Benjamin was, he had heard of her. Her name evoked the same feeling that the vampire Malachi's did.

Shaking his head, he muttered, "Stop creating trouble where there is none. Wait and see what happens. See if she truly is gifted before you start planning."

He was also trying to fool himself.

Oh, she was a witch all right.

And an Inherent.

But somehow, she had kept herself from changing.

Somehow she had suppressed her magick.

Or somebody had done it for her. From beyond the grave, perhaps?

For years.

She was the daughter of Carrick Wallace, one of Declan O'Reilly's father's right-hand men. He and Adrienne had been murdered and their young daughter had gone missing twenty-three years ago. After Declan had walked away so many years before, the pack had reformed, restructured, and had executed the rogues.

They had searched high and low for Shadoe Wallace, the young babe mourned by so many.

And that child was Jillian, the woman who had fought off two rogue shape-shifters, a werewolf and an Inherent, and killed one of them.

She had done time in jail for protecting herself when she should have been coddled and praised, loved, adored, worshipped—shit, it made him furious just thinking of it. If he had found her just a little sooner, none of it would have happened.

Hell, maybe he was wrong. Maybe she wasn't an Inherent in truth. How could she have resisted the call of the moon, the call of the hunt, the magick of feeling the Wolf's call for more than a decade?

She may not be a true shape-shifter, but she was more than human now.

He just had to figure out exactly what she was.

And soon. Before their enemies arrived.

* * * * *

The dream came again… *Struggling on the floor, screaming as he lunged at her, biting with a face that seemed to shift and change and grow as his teeth sank into the mound of her right breast, tearing away flesh and branding her, hot waves of blood streaming from the bloody little hole. Then the stranger, his weight crashing down —*

Jillian forced herself to wake up, gasping for air. The remnants of the dream were stark and clear. For the first time ever.

"He bit me," she said slowly. *Why haven't I remembered that before now?* She jerked the vee neckline of the men's shirt she slept in aside, and stared down at her breast, at the smooth flesh of it. It had never borne a mark. Not now, not the morning she woke in the hospital under arrest, the day after she had killed Jimmy.

"I'm losing my mind," she whispered, shaking her head, running her fingers over the smooth flesh. She could *remember* it, the tearing, searing agony of it, the pain, the hot wash of blood, the pleasure in Jimmy's eyes, and his thirst for more. The ragged, bloody hole where he had torn the flesh away from her body.

But there was no mark. If he had truly bitten her, she would have carried that scar for life.

And his face couldn't possibly have been changing the way she remembered.

It just wasn't possible.

So she was losing her mind.

"Ms. Morgan."

She went stiff.

Jillian knew that deep, almost growling voice. That voice had fueled a couple of very *interesting* dreams during the long, empty years in jail.

Benjamin Cross. Slowly she turned and met a pair of golden-brown eyes across a distance of a few feet. She hadn't even considered that he would try approaching her. And now she realized just how foolish that had been. His persistence had known no bounds, so why had she suddenly expected that to change?

"I've no desire to speak with you, Mr. Cross. I do not give interviews," she said firmly, stifling the urge to stare as she gazed upon the man who had been calling her on a monthly basis for five years.

The phone calls had started within a month of her incarceration. At first, he'd just offered to come in and speak with her about her ordeal. Then he'd offered to "interview" her for a book deal. Then he'd offered to interview her regarding her books. Although how he had discovered *that* piece of knowledge, she didn't know. Then he'd just started calling to pester her.

Politely. Always politely.

But the phone calls never stopped.

A year into her sentence, letters had started coming, along with research books on magick and shape-shifters, and ghosts. The majority of her better books had in fact come from the man staring at her with those mesmerizing golden eyes.

Holy hell. It was a damn good thing she hadn't known what he looked like, otherwise she just might have given in to those interviews. Just for writer's curiosity, mind you...but *damn.*

His dark brown hair fell into his eyes in loose waves and he absently brushed it back with a lean, tanned hand, cocking his head and studying her intently. "You didn't really think I would just up and leave you alone, did you?" he asked, curiously.

She had the odd impression of a pup staring at her with his ears pricked. Or a wolf... Shaking her head, she focused on a point just beyond his shoulder and said, "Actually I hadn't thought of it." Her eyes cut back to him as she added, "Or you."

"Ouch," he said mildly, those amazing eyes dancing with humor.

Of course, if she had known what he looked like... *Oh, that would have been torture in there*, she thought helplessly.

Underneath the green chamois shirt he wore, there was a ribbed undershirt that stretched across his wide chest, his skin gleaming gold, muscles clearly evident beneath the clinging fabric. Worn jeans clung to his lean hips and long, muscled thighs as Jillian cursed her peripheral vision and forced herself to meet his eyes.

They looked...hot, hungry... A smell assaulted her senses, the smell of lust and the primal need to mate. Though how she could place such a name to that hot, musky scent, she didn't know. Any more than she could figure out how she could smell it so clearly.

Hell, his eyes—gleaming, glowing... The striations in his eyes were starting to swirl and shift...

Unbeknownst to her, a soft whimper escaped her as she stared hypnotized into those eyes. She had seen eyes like that once upon a time and fear arced through her. A gasp fell from her lips and she retreated, her eyes wide and unblinking on his face.

And as she watched, the look left his eyes, his lids drooped, the odd tension seemed to leave him, and a gentle smile curved his mouth, the full lower lip curving just slightly. "I'm no threat to *you*, Jillian Morgan," he said softly, his voice intense. "To those who threaten you, I bring death — slow and painful — but I am no threat to you, ever."

He turned and left.

* * * * *

Ben had to force down the rage.

She had more of their kind inside of her than he had suspected. She had scented his hunger — it was too much like Marcus', and she didn't know Ben. It had frightened her, the sharp, biting scent that had filled the air all around her, making her slim body go stiff and her pretty blue eyes go wild.

And the scent of magick had strengthened. Witch. She had witch in her as well, how much, how powerful, he wouldn't know until he got closer, touched her, searched her. Jillian had been suppressing the magick, and the wolf, for so long... She had pushed it deep. Or her mother had.

He was starting to suspect it was the latter. Adrienne had been oh so powerful. And very desperate, he imagined, to protect her young babe.

Stalking around his car, he waited a moment before climbing in. He didn't want to drive. He wanted to run...to hunt...to attack...

His hands clenched into tight fists as he lifted his head to the sky, the ends of his dark brown hair waving in the soft breeze as he battled against the rage and hunger in him.

The wind blew, bringing with it a familiar scent, and he growled menacingly. Marcus. He wasn't here. Not now. The scent was old. Days old. The rogue Inherent was stalking Jillian again.

"Know this, Marcus. This time, you will die." Sliding his eyes to the store, he felt a shudder roll through his body as he tamped down the urge to shift as a familiar friend raised his head and whispered, *Shall we go Hunting, my friend?*

Ben smiled tightly as he closed his hand into a fist, banishing the wild power of the change as he responded to the Wolf. "No. There is nothing there to Hunt right now. My duty lies here."

The Wolf chuffed and Ben laughed slightly as he slid into the truck. "I got us this far, didn't I?"

There was no comment from the ancient creature as he settled back into whatever resting space a totem spirit called home, but Ben could feel his mirth. Shaking his head, he settled back to wait on Jillian.

* * * * *

To those who threaten you, I bring death — slow and painful — but I am no threat to you, ever.

Jillian didn't understand exactly why those words brought her comfort. But they did.

"I am totally sick," she muttered to herself as she slid her groceries into the car.

The more she thought about his words, the more they disturbed her. But not that way... They should have frightened her, because she could feel the raw energy inside the man, and knew damned well he could — and would — make good on that threat.

Violence repelled her... So why did those words disturb her for all the wrong reasons? And in all the wrong ways.

In the best possible, most delicious way imaginable. Squirming on her seat, she bit her lip and started the engine.

"I am *not* going to get turned on just because of what he said," she whispered, shaking her head.

A naughty little voice in her head whispered, *Then do it because he's so damn hot.*

An image of him surfaced in her mind, that wind-tossed brown hair tumbling into those golden eyes, his skin dusky, that sexy five o'clock shadow that was so enticing on a man. Big shoulders, brawny and wide, a chest she suspected would feel oh so nice, under her head, and powerful arms, a flat belly...

Her writer's imagination kicked into play as she recalled just how *hot* he was.

Jillian smothered a laugh and laid her head on the steering wheel of the car, snorting in laughter. "Oh, man. I've lost my mind."

After snickering to herself for a few minutes, she sighed, and just rested there. Safe. Something about him had made her feel *safe* for the briefest instant. That was incredibly freeing.

Lifting her head up, she focused on the drive back home. And another long, empty, sleepless night.

She couldn't sleep without the nightmares plaguing her.

* * * * *

Ben prowled the town.

Marcus' scent was there. And more wolves. Tilting his head back, he drew the scents in, remembering them, filing them away. A wolf pack in this town... That wasn't right.

There were no wolves around here. At least, there shouldn't be. There was a pack a few hours north of here, a pack populated with free-roaming Hunters. No packs were allowed to settle without letting the Council know.

It was law.

And there was a Master Vamp an hour to the south, with a well-situated enclave that would patrol even this far away at least every few weeks.

No pack would move into an area so already laden with weres and vamps, so many of them Hunters. It was foolishness. And to break the law?

But he scented at least five different wolves as he moved through the area. In a town as small as this? Five wolves living together and not knowing the other wasn't likely. Thus, a pack.

One that disregarded old law courtesy by failing to let the northern pack know of their presence. One that didn't give a damn about the Master living to the south.

No. That was certain foolishness.

Or worse. If they were here because of Jillian, then that meant Marcus was up to no good.

Of course, the rogue had been up to pure evil for years. Hunting him was a damn near impossible task. Inherent rogues just shouldn't be allowed. The instincts of an Inherent made him so much more difficult to track, especially when he traveled alone.

Ben knew, because he'd been tracking Marcus for years, ever since he'd seen the headlines and that picture of Jillian and known, *finally*, his search for Shadoe Wallace was over.

He'd had to divide his time between trying to woo her trust, which had failed miserably, and searching for Marcus.

But the search was over—Marcus had come to him.

And he would pay.

* * * * *

Jillian's eyes opened.

She forced her breathing to remain even, out of sheer instinct—the knowledge we all carry inside us, that if we move, if we breathe, the predator will hear us.

There was somebody in her house.

Breathing slowly through her nose, she scented something…rich. Like the woods at night. And something foul, like death lurking in those woods. There was no sound, not a squeaking floorboard, nor a breath of a sigh.

But there was somebody in her house.

Marcus?

"I hear your heartbeat, wolf. I know you're awake," a soft lilting voice called. "Come on out…do not make this troublesome. Marcus will be angered if we tarry too long."

A woman?

Slowly, Jillian slid from the bed, her eyes on the door. The fear inside her had her heart racing, and she forced herself to take a deep breath and let it out through her nose. *Calm…be calm. In the face of our enemies, we show no fear. It feeds them.*

Jillian stifled the urge to laugh hysterically. That damn voice… It sounded so very real, and so familiar.

But her heartbeat slowed. She could actually feel it as she walked backward to the window. There was only one inside. Straining, she tried to listen for a sound outside, concentrating…focusing…

An odd image drifted in front of her eyes and she saw two men. One at the front door. Another at the back.

Caging her in.

Damn it.

Oh, shit…somebody help me, she thought desperately, never taking her eyes from the door.

Good girl, the soft, soothing voice whispered. *He's coming…*

Jillian's heart skittered to a stop. *He's coming? As in Marcus?*

"I won't go through that again," she said aloud, her voice flat and firm. "I won't. I'll kill you first. I'll die first."

A lilting laugh sounded through the house and Jillian knew the woman was on the stairs now.

"*Chére,* you don't have a choice," the woman said in a cheerful, easy voice.

Open your heart. Open your soul. The knowledge is there, safe and secure where I put it all those years ago…open…

Open…

Open…

Jillian's entire body was trembling and there was a cynical voice in the back of her mind, whispering, *You've lost your mind, Jilly. Totally gone…*

Then the voice became firm and it said strongly, *Your name isn't Jillian. It's Shadoe, and you are not insane. You are my daughter and you can fight this. Now, do it. Open yourself…*

Jillian felt something inside her break and shift.

Wind whipped through the room. Her eyes moved to the window. It wasn't open. Her breath froze in her throat and she stared at the door. She shouldn't have been able to see it so well. It was so dark… *Need light…damn it, how can I fight if I can't see?*

Light blazed out of nowhere. Jillian had to blink at the brightness of it. She searched for a source. Where had it come from? The lamp was off, and the light over her bed was off. Staring around, she saw that everything she looked at was in pure, bright focus. And when she turned her gaze away, it fell into the shadows.

The light was *her.*

And it was burning.

* * * * *

Benjamin felt the desperate plea as though she whispered it in his ear. Coming out of the shadows, a snarl rumbled from his throat as he caught the scent of the wolves nearly two miles away.

"Marcus…" he rasped as he felt the change tear through him, vicious and uncontrolled. He slammed one clawed hand against the trunk of a tree and fought the howl rising in his throat as the muscles inside his body shifted and changed, a flow of fur covering once golden, gleaming skin. His eyes gleamed yellow-gold in the dark as he rose to the full height of his wolfman form and took off running, following the scent of her fear, the scent of wild magick that was brewing in the air.

They hadn't been expecting that, he imagined.

Or him. *Touch her, Marcus…and pay the price.*

The magick was breaking open inside her, spurred by her fear, and as he lunged over the thick growth of bushes surrounding her home, he caught the scent of wolf. Inherent…female…sweet. The wolf was starting to wake within her as well. *Fuck. She can't handle both right now.*

As he hit her street, everything around him a blur from his speed, he focused and reached out. At his touch, the anxious animal, hovering just beyond her subconscious, calmed as he forced his own will upon it.

He slowed to a prowl as he came to her house, sliding his eyes to the man guarding the front door and smiled as the wolf inside Jillian seemed to retreat, confused, frightened, but recognizing the power of the Inherent controlling his ward's wolven instincts.

He then slid his gaze to the werewolf who only now realized he had company. The bonds he kept wrapped around the Wolf's power, the power of fear, fell away and he stalked around as the man's eyes went black with fear, and a urine stain appeared on the front of his jeans.

"Marcus didn't prepare you for me, did he?" Ben growled, reaching out and raking one wicked, deadly talon down the werewolf's cheek, drawing blood. "Didn't he realize I was here?"

A whimper, like that of a puppy, fell from the man's throat and he gasped, "Please—I only obey my Master!"

"Even if it involves the rape, abuse, and torture of the innocent," Ben asked, staring down at the small, human male. The man tried to change, tried to summon the power of the full moon only a day away and Ben laughed, dousing the summons before it could truly form. "Pitiful, don't you know better? I *own* you. So pathetic."

The man fell to his knees sobbing and pleaded, "Don't fucking kill me, Inherent."

Ben knelt, the silken pelt of fur covering his long, powerful body gleaming softly, the muscles in his shifted form bunching and knotting as he moved.

"Oh, I won't. That is too easy," he promised, reaching out with his clawed hand and gathering the blood on the bastard's cheek. "You get to face the Council. And live out your years locked inside your body, unable to shift, unable to hunt. Until the needs and hungers inside you destroy your mind and your body."

At the words The Council, the man panicked and screamed. "No—"

With a whisper the entrapment spell settled into place around the werewolf and he fell silent, unable to move, to blink.

"There now. All wrapped tight, and bound to me, for now. And once you face the Council, that spell will be changed to one where you can't ever run, can't ever hunt again."

Rising, Ben faced the door and kicked it in, snarling and hungry for blood. Halfway up the stairs, he shifted from his wolven form and made himself calm, sucking in air desperately as the shift completed, leaving him naked and full of rage.

"…not fighting," a laughing woman said. "There is no point to fighting. You can't possibly hope to win."

Ben moved into the doorway and asked calmly, "Why not?"

The female werewolf's eyes flew to his face and she screeched, "Jude! Michael!"

"Hmmm… Jude can't help you," Ben said, a smile curving his lips. "Neither can the others, but if you think screaming will help…"

Turning his gaze from the wolf, he said quietly. "Jillian. Let it go. Stop fighting what is inside you."

Then he turned to face the charging werewolf who had come to answer the rogue's scream, leaving Jillian alone to battle the female.

Whatever was twisting inside her was wild, raw, and alive. It writhed and burned with a life of its own. Clamping it down now was out of the question, so she just had to release it.

* * * * *

Jillian heard his deep, insistent voice echoing inside her head as she stared at the slender, almost delicate woman in front of her. *Stop fighting what is inside you…*

Lifting one hand, she stared at it, at the gleaming ivory flesh that glowed from within, her breath coming in ragged pants before she lifted her eyes to the woman.

"This is my home. Get out," she snapped.

The woman laughed, a desperate, evil laugh. "No can do. He wants you. He will have you. And I won't fail him," she hissed.

Jillian fought the storm that was raging inside her. *He…he… Who is she talking about?* Jillian thought as she stared at the woman.

The image seemed to explode from the woman's mind into Jillian's, burning itself into her mind's eye.

Marcus…

"Over my dead body," Jillian cried, flinging one hand to the woman who was dropping into a crouch, preparing to lunge. Jillian could see it, the shadow of an animal lurking inside the depths of the woman's eyes. The bitch would kill her if she could, but alive was better. Alive was pleasing to Marcus.

With her hand raised, she screamed, "No!"

The heat inside her exploded and Jillian couldn't control it as it arced out of her hand and seemed to grab at the intruder, winding around her flesh like a lover, setting flame to her hair, her clothes, her very body.

A scream echoed through the air and the smell of burning cotton filled the air, the heat scorching her as Jillian stood there, now facing the blazing, burning form of the werewolf, shock and fear and disbelief racing through Jillian as she stumbled back against the wall, the burning hot energy that had filled her now gone.

"Enough," a soft, gentle voice said.

Jillian quivered as Benjamin Cross walked naked through the door and lifted one hand just in front of the smoldering, flaming corpse in front of her. The husk fell to the ground and Benjamin stepped around it as the fire died, winking out of existence…as though he had made the fire die.

"I did."

Jillian couldn't stop the whimper that fell from her lips. Gently, he smiled and said, "No threat to you."

Then he stepped a little closer and said, "Welcome back, Shadoe Wallace. You've been hiding a very long time."

Shadoe…

Images assaulted her mind—almost memories—a short, stocky man with a close-cut beard and laughing eyes, and a slender fey creature with hands that soothed and gentled. *Shadoe, my pretty little Shadoe…isn't she beautiful, Carrick?* Voices with the lilting music of Ireland inside them…tears thickened her throat and she pressed her lips together as a dull, rushing sound filled her ears. Jillian stared at Ben, quivering as the images became too real, too vivid. "What in the hell is going on?" she demanded, then flinched as her voice echoed and boomed through the small bedroom.

"Come to me, Shadoe. There is so much you need to know," Benjamin said, holding out his hand.

Wildly, she shook her head and moved further away, feeling the wall against her back as the spicy, bitter taste of fear tore through her, adrenaline starting to course through her veins.

Her fear was spiraling out of control and she couldn't stop it, couldn't think, couldn't breathe…

Jillian didn't realize he had moved closer, until one hand was cupping her cheek. *"Not yet,"* a voice whispered in her mind.

"Come down, I'll catch you."

Jillian gasped and stumbled into his arms as a black fog rose and obscured her vision, taking her thoughts, her fears, her everything with it.

Chapter Two

Benjamin laid her on the bed, stroking her hair back from her face. "Pretty girl, you've been through hell, haven't you?" he murmured, the fury still twisting in his gut.

But, damn…didn't she do good?

Pure, raw, unrefined magick was coursing through her veins now, the well of power inside her wide open. It wouldn't be closed off again.

And such a loud, bitter awakening she'd received.

"Sorry for that, sweet," he whispered, his gaze moving to the smoking corpse feet away.

Clean up.

Clean up first, then sit and wonder what to do about the pretty young witchling, he told himself.

Two corpses and a sniveling, magickally bound wolf in the foyer, out of sight of passersby. He paused long enough to thank the good Lord that Shadoe didn't live in town. It would have been very hard to explain away the screams, the blinding lights that poured from Shadoe's body as her magick erupted.

Shadoe. Closing his eyes, he muttered, "She might not like you changing her name."

It was nearly an hour later when he had finished dealing with the mess. Not just the bodies, but the blood.

Neither soap and water, nor bleach could take the bloodstains off the wall, so he hadn't bothered. Magick, however, could.

Most of the time was spent *talking*, however.

Two phone calls made, one to the Master in the south, the other to the pack in the north to let them know they had a rogue pack preying in the small town of Cruthersville, caught between the pack's town of Buxton and the Master's native Biloxi.

The pack leader would deal with the corpses, he was told, after much hot and heavy swearing, then worried questions…

No. I do not believe this pack is something you are responsible for. No. Do not send investigators down. I will kill this one…

And the Master's icy fury wasn't much better.

Both of the powerful creatures now worried that the Council would come seeking them, and it had taken some time to convince them that he was the Council's voice here right now, and he saw nothing at fault with them.

Even though they were Hunters—or maybe because they were, their fears had been raised. Perhaps the Council would make them pay for not discovering the rogue pack?

Hell, Hunters weren't omniscient—even if they had been a bit lax in their duties. That wasn't, however, cause for the Council to come visiting.

Of course, he didn't mind the pack doing the cleanup.

That kept him from having to deal with the corpses.

He did, however, need a Hunter to escort their baggage to the Council. Somebody to watch over the pathetic, mewling wolf who still clung to the wall, begging, "Don't kill me…"

Tossing him a disgusted look, he said, "If you don't be silent, I will. And may God forgive me."

A Hunter who wouldn't kill his sorry ass just for existing. That would be difficult. This whining whelp would sorely try even the most patient Hunter… Ben stopped mid-step.

Or he could just kill two birds with one stone. There was another witch he needed to get to the Council. One who wouldn't go on her own, but just might go to help another. A woman who had eyes almost as sad as Shadoe's, and every bit as tortured.

Crossing to the mirror hanging at the southern wall, he brushed his fingers over it, letting some of his blood smear the reflection as he sent the summons out. She didn't answer right away, but he really hadn't expected her to.

Leandra was fighting her fate, tooth and nail.

* * * * *

Shadoe...prettiest little Shadoe, a laughing, gruff voice said.

She could feel hands, big, loving hands lifting her up and cuddling her against a broad, warm chest. She felt warm, safe, secure.

And so loved.

Another voice, sweet and soft, but firm... "Carrick, you are going to spoil that girl rotten. I mean it, no more candy." Then soft and loving hands pinching her chin lightly, a soft laugh. "Don't pout so, Shadoe. 'Tis bedtime, that is all, love. You can't eat candy in bed, baby."

The same voice, singing her to sleep at night.

And then there was terror, screaming, struggling, burning... "Adri, get the baby. Get out..." That deep man's voice ordering, his tone brooking no disobedience.

"I can't leave you!"

A ferocious snarl and the sound of breaking glass. "They have me trapped, a blood spell, I can feel it. Do you want her to die as well as me?"

The soft, lovely voice sobbing. "No. Our babe can't die...she's too important. Oh, Shadoe...forgive us!"

Hot swirling mists seemed to fill the baby, flood her, muffling her voice, and her soul. "Adri, take her and go!"

"No," the woman said, her voice calmer now. "They can track me too easily. They know my scent, my blood."

"She needs a protector, damn it. You know what can happen to a magicked baby in the world. One scent of her blood, of the wolf inside her, once it emerges. *Go!*"

A few moments passed and the baby Shadoe had felt something wrench the air, and a woman's furious shriek. "Damn *them!*"

Then the muffling, hot power, like the electricity in the air during a furious storm, continued to soak in Jillian...no, Shadoe. Her real name was Shadoe and the woman who held her, who kissed her cheek and sang softly, only replied to the man. "I can't. Don't you think I've tried? I can't. Not because I won't leave you, although it would near kill me. They locked me to you. I cannot go where you cannot follow. They've killed us, Carrick, both of us."

That furious snarl—hot, snapping rage—filled the room and a baby whimpered. "Shhh, my pretty Shadoe. Our pretty Shadoe. Damn it, Adri. We can't let them kill her," a tortured, angry man rasped. Shadoe felt his hands stroke down her hair, her small, shaking back.

"They won't. They won't even know where to look for her," the woman said.

Mama...my mama...mine... The words formed in Shadoe's mind, more than two decades later as she lay trapped in the dream, the memory that had been buried inside her.

"You will be *safe*," Mama whispered. Something warm and wet splattered on Shadoe's face. "My blood, my power, my tears...my offering to the Lord. Protect her. And hide the power that will show her nature—until the time comes for all to know."

"Adri, what are you doing?"

"What we have to do, love."

Shadoe passed into strong arms and was clasped to that broad chest, a whisker-roughened face pressed against her tiny cheek as he kissed her gently. "My prettiest Shadoe, damn it, I love you. In your heart, know that, baby," he said.

Daddy... "Yes, it's Daddy, now gimme kisses, pretty girl, and then hug your mama tight," he crooned, that big strong hand that had always protected, stroking down her back.

"It's time," Mama whispered, her voice muffled, tight. "Aww, my angel. My Shadoe. It's all right. It will be all right…all in time…"

And then something inside the young girl known as Shadoe went out.

And she awoke. Twenty-six years old, and now remembering her true parents' faces.

"Mama," she choked.

"She suppressed the magick. Did what she had to. Your parents were—"

Shadoe sat up and turned her head, staring at Benjamin Cross in the darkened room. "How do you know me?" she asked, her voice trembling.

A tired, sad smile crossed his face. "Your parents had family, friends, who searched endlessly for you. I've been looking for years. And when I found you, it was too late to keep something bad from happening. Marcus had caught your scent, your magick… It started coming out. If the magick had just waited—ah, that will get nothing accomplished. The rest you know. You were in jail when I arrived. And you wouldn't even consent to see me, so I could see if it was really you," he said as he moved out of the shadows, dropping to his knees beside her bed.

"That's not an answer. How do you know me? Who am I?" she demanded, lifting her hands and staring at them. "How did I do that? What is going on inside me?"

"You know who you are now, I think. Your name is Shadoe Wallace," he said. "And you are one helluva powerful witch. That is what kept Jimmy and Marcus from killing you that night. That is what saved you tonight. The magick your mother hid inside your body has broken free, love."

Magick.

As if the word itself were magickal, Shadoe felt something like a blindfold, fall away, and she could *see*. Far too much. Staring at Benjamin Cross too hard made his body gleam with a blue light, and when she jerked her head around to stare outside, shimmery, darting bits of energy seemed to infuse the trees, the air, the very night.

She could feel the sheets below her, almost each individual thread of the smooth sateen. Each stray hair as it caressed her cheek.

And his heart. She could hear his heart. Smell his skin, hot, warm, male. Smell the wildness of a thunderstorm, the woodsy pine scent of the forest, of sandalwood and sage and man. Saliva flooded her mouth and she felt a dam break open in her belly, moisture flooding her cleft as she breathed in his scent, an almost electric caress of air on her body.

"What is going on...?" she asked, terror filling her, control sliding far and fast from her grip.

"It's you, what you really are, your magick coming out," he said gruffly, his voice strained. "You have no idea what has been hiding behind the veil of your mother's protection. Have mercy, your scent..."

Her gaze flew to his face and she saw his eyes, those golden eyes were glowing, gold and amber streaks that swirled and danced around his pupils. They were locked on her face, sending hot, skittering little rushes down her back, jolts of electricity that had her clenching her thighs together.

He closed his eyes, and shook his head. She could see—something—seem to fade from him, drifting from his flesh like fairy dust. "You are a witch, Shadoe Wallace, and much more. And it's all coming out now. The power of what you have inside could drive a lesser person mad," he said obliquely as his eyes opened.

"Who are you? Why are you here?" Shadoe asked, hearing the desperate ring in her voice, and unable to silence it.

He smiled, a sardonic twist of his lips. "I came to find *you*," he said simply. "And I will be whoever you want me to be. Although I hope, for your sake, a teacher is what you wish of me. Because that light inside you will never go out again."

* * * * *

Leandra stared at the mirror over the sink in the small, ramshackle cabin in Slade, Kentucky.

In this tiny, pretty country town, she had found a little bit of peace. And it had just been broken.

"Damned Hunters, all of dem," she whispered huskily. Her hands clenched at the edge of the sink and she closed her eyes tightly. She had gone out west, to New Mexico and they had known her.

She had spent a year in Milan. And they had known her.

Everywhere she went, the damned Hunters knew her name, her scent, her magick.

But she no longer saw hatred or disgust in their eyes. Over the past few years it had changed. To pity.

Pity!

"I don't need deir pity," she snarled, her head whipping up as she stared at her reflection, looking into the tortured eyes that they saw, no doubt.

Then what do you need… a gentle voice asked.

Lost in the pain of her past, she slumped, and her brow rested against the mirror, without her truly realizing.

The magick of Cross' spell leaped to life, activated by her touch and his deep, gravelly voice filled the room, gentle, but hard at the same time. "You need a purpose, Leandra, warrior witch. How long will you fight what you are meant to be?"

Jerking her head back, Leandra swore heatedly. "Damn ya, Cross. Go away. Leave me be," she hissed, backing away as she stared into his opaque, golden eyes.

Not Cross…*please*, not him. He had been the hardest to ignore, when he had come seeking her out. Not telling her that she had a duty, not ordering her into training, like some fools had done. He had looked at her and simply said, "Aren't you tired of not being where you belong?"

Yes.

She had bitten that answer back. But as he met her gaze levelly, she knew he had seen it written all over her face. Leandra had fled to Milan after that.

His laughter drew her back into the present. "They have been leaving you be for years. It's been nearly four years since you walked away from the evil. It never truly touched *you*, never took its hold, yet you still let it rule you. Why?"

She laughed harshly. "I am evil, Cross. A witch of de Scythe. The only one left, don't ya know? I *am* evil."

Ben sighed and the sound seemed to fill the room around her. "You don't have an evil bone in that very lovely body, Leandra. Full of guilt, anger, pain, yes. But you are not evil. And the Scythe are not dead. Just one small sect."

"You're wrong," she shouted. "Lori killed dem. They all died under de mountain she pulled down on dem."

"That one small sect," Ben agreed. "They did indeed die. But they are not our only enemies. And the Scythe still lives. The Mistress had the most powerful young sect growing. But hers was just one seed. The Scythe will spread like a forest over the land unless we stop it."

Leandra felt a quivering deep inside her, a fury unlike any she had ever known. "Dey still live?" she rasped as blue flame shot and sparked around her hands. In the past four years, Leandra had searched, had studied, had learned. So many faces she had seen come into the Scythe, for such a brief time. Young ones, confused, angry teenagers, lost, desperate children, women with no place to turn.

And she had never seen them more than a handful of times.

But she had felt them as she'd traveled the places the Scythe had roamed before making their home in West Virginia. And her travels had revealed exactly what had happened to those lost, angry souls.

Now truly lost…dead, graves scattered here and there, a trail of missing persons everywhere they had gone.

Harvesting and claiming the power of the innocent, the desperate, looking for recruits, for victims. For food.

"You have hidden long enough, Leandra," Benjamin said softly. "Come out now. We need you."

That simple plea, stated so very basically, hit home. Leandra touched the mirror with a shaking hand, breaking the spell, making his face go away.

You have hidden long enough.

We need you…

Damn it, even that bastard Malachi hadn't bothered her so badly. And he had pestered her for nearly a month in Milan before he had given up. Of course, she had finally threatened him with a volley of fireballs, so that might have been why he left.

Not that she had actually tried to hit him—she just had to get him away from her. The longer he was around, the more she was tempted to listen to him, that soft sexy burr, the compassion she saw in his midnight eyes.

Of course, Cross didn't even have to be around her. With that uncanny intuition, he had known *exactly* what to say to make her think, make her question…

Make her yearn.

Not for him, although he was a fine creature, indeed.

But to *belong*, to be where she was meant to be. For the longest time, she had been convinced that she had no place in the world…not now.

But with just a few gruffly spoken words, and understanding in his golden eyes, he had made her question what little she had left to believe.

Damn bastard, she thought, pacing the room.

Damn him to hell.

With a smirk, she thought, *At least, then I won't be so damned lonely…*

Chapter Three

"I am not a witch," Shadoe said somberly, staring at the brooding, sexy man in front of her. "Magick isn't real. What I thought I saw happen the night Jimmy died isn't real."

A sigh left his lips. "How long will you fight the truth? What is it with you women? So blind to the truth. To fact." He turned away, running a long-fingered hand through his tumbled hair, the shirt he had gotten from somewhere stretching across those wide shoulders with the absent gesture.

"Fact? Magick can't be fact! It's not logical. Fire can't come out of thin air," she argued, shaking her head and backing away from him as he turned back around to stare at her, a tiny smile on his face.

"Why not?" he asked reasonably, crossing his arms over his chest. Cocking a brow at her, he said, "It's not like a normal person is doing it. It's a witch. There are laws to it, just like with everything else. You take the wild energy in the air that comes from every living creature and you combust it. It's perfectly logical. For crying out loud, listen to your head. It will tell you the truth. It tells you that you are a witch... It tells you that you can make fire, that you *have* made fire."

"How can I possibly believe what my head is telling me?" Shadoe shouted, stomping away from him, staring out the window into the night. Taking a deep breath, she said quietly, "So maybe I did dream of my parents. But that doesn't make me a fucking witch. That doesn't mean I made fire."

She froze in mid-track as Ben lifted one hand. "If you are not a witch, then neither am I," he said casually. "But how can I do this?"

Shadoe's eyes were trapped on the golden orb that Benjamin held. Locked on the two faces within it, faces that were distantly familiar, and a knot rose in her throat. Her parents… A short pixie-like woman with a head full of wild red curls, chopped to chin-length, cuddled up against a blond Viking, a goatee on his face. They were staring down at a baby the woman held cuddled against her… *That's me…*

As she stared, mesmerized, the child grew to a chubby little toddler who latched her hands onto Mama's curls and laughed as her father tickled her. "I know them," Shadoe whispered thickly, fighting the tears that threatened to fall.

"I know them," she repeated as memory flooded her and tears stung her eyes. She remembered a slide, and a park, and a puppy…and them, the man and the woman, always the man and the woman, their voices, and the love in their hands, and in their voices.

"How could I have forgotten?"

"You had to, Shadoe," he murmured, holding still as she reached out with a shaky hand to touch the images locked within the orb.

Her hand slid right through it and she jerked it back, clamping her lips together to keep from crying out in shock as the man turned his head and stared directly out at her, as though he could see her.

The man had the bluest of eyes, pure, clear sky blue. Shadoe was looking into her own eyes as she said, "I have his eyes. How are you doing this? I *know* them."

"Your heart never forgot, Shadoe. Yes, you have his eyes. Much of him within you. Just like you have so much of your mother," Benjamin said quietly. "Power runs heavy in your blood, Shadoe. As it does in mine."

Hypnotized, she lifted her hand to touch the orb again, her fingers passing through, splintering it. She fought the urge to cry as their faces faded away. "I don't have any power in my blood," she argued, shaking her head. She could accept her parents, wanted to, even.

But the rest?

Benjamin arched a brow and stepped through the shimmering bits of energy that still hung in the air after the orb had shattered under her touch. "You *are* power, sweet," he murmured, reaching down and taking her hand, locking their fingers together and staring into her troubled blue eyes.

Shadoe felt something explode from her, as though leaping out to meet Benjamin, joining with his power. She felt it, a resounding hum that filled her very soul, flooding her from the top of her head to the soles of her feet. And her skin was gleaming again. A ragged gasp fell from her lips and she lifted her hands, staring at them, watching as the rich, gleaming flesh seemed to glow and shine. She turned her head and stared at her reflection in the mirror, seeing the deep, gleaming pools of her eyes.

A harsh male groan echoed in her ears and she tore her eyes away from her reflection to stare at Ben, the muscles in her belly tightening at the hungry look in his eyes, etched onto his face.

"I'd kill him again," Benjamin whispered, reaching out and trailing one finger down her cheek. "The bastard who dared to hurt you. I'd happily kill him again. I hate death, yet I wish to see his happen over and over again for putting the briefest moment of fear into your life." A menacing growl, something that was totally not human, fell from his lips as he moved a little closer. "And Marcus—he will die. I crave his death, almost as much as…"

Shadoe's heart skipped as he lowered his head, cupping her face in his hands, lifting her mouth and taking it hungrily, pushing his tongue—hot, rough and seductive—into her mouth. One hand threaded through her hair and she sobbed as he moved his body against her, bringing his heat, so seductively necessary that Shadoe wondered how she had ever lived without it. He held himself back, touching her with just one hand in her hair, his mouth on hers, his other hand gripping her hip, strong and firm. Shadoe gasped as a shudder racked that big body and she was pulled completely against him, his chest crushing her breasts, a flat, hard belly coming to rest against the softness of hers.

He seemed to fill her, some intangible energy from him sliding inside her and filling all the dark, empty places she had lived with for so long.

Ben's mouth ate at hers, his tongue rubbing seductively against hers, before he pulled back. Nipping her lower lip, he let his lips cruise down the line of her neck. A big hand, firm and hard, came up to her breast and Shadoe whimpered when he pinched the nipple lightly, teasingly as he lowered his mouth to feast on the other.

Cool air kissed her flesh and she cried out as she felt him tear the shirt away only seconds before the hot, wet silk of his mouth closed over her nipple. Drawing it deep, laving it roughly, he nipped at her again, rolling his eyes upward to stare at her face.

His eyes—so intent, so rapt on her face. Shadoe felt her knees buckle and his big hands caught her, bringing her into the air as he licked and bit and sucked on her. Her head fell back and she arched against the hot length between her thighs, instinctively wrapping her legs around Ben's waist and arching, rubbing against him.

"Well, now… Dat is not de sight I expected t' see."

Benjamin snarled, tearing his mouth from Shadoe's sweet flesh as that soft, mocking voice filled the room. So damn caught up in the sweetness of her, in her unexpectedly fiery response that Leandra was able to fly into the room without him even feeling her.

Damn it, Malachi had pegged her as a flier, but Benjamin hadn't really considered it, until the long, sleekly built Jamaican appeared in the room within a span of heartbeats.

Leandra moved across the room, her eyes focused and controlled, and lowered herself lazily into a chair. Her pale amber eyes flashed at them.

"Ever heard of knocking?" he asked drolly.

Shadoe yelped, her eyes shocked, wide and watchful, on Leandra's face. "What are you doing here?" she rasped, her mouth still swollen, hot from his touch. "Who in the hell are you? And how did you get into my house?"

Leandra smirked. "Ask de wolfboy. He is the one who called me," she replied, tossing the man behind Shadoe a sardonic glare. "Where is dis bastard I need to take to the Council?"

"Leandra, lovely manners as always," he said tightly, stroking his hand through Shadoe's tumbled hair before setting her on her feet and stepping back. "This is Shadoe Wallace," he murmured, still staring into her eyes, those clear, indignant eyes.

The taste of her lingered in his mouth and he battled down the need to take...*and take...and take...*

Swallowing, he turned his head away from her before his control shattered. "Ahhh... Well, she may prefer to be called Jillian. She's been known as Jillian Morgan for more than twenty years."

The air was sparking.

Three powerful witches in such proximity, though Leandra and Benjamin had their magick tamped down deep inside them, Shadoe's was dancing in the air like dust motes.

Leandra drew one long, black-clad leg to her chest and inclined her head. "Formalities done, Benjamin Cross. Where is de nasty little wolf ya want me to watch? And why ask me? I be no Hunter," she said, her voice low, easy, but still not one Benjamin could ignore.

"That is only from your own stubbornness. They want you. Badly," he said, taking a deep, sighing breath and forcing the hunger back inside him. Not now...he couldn't have Shadoe now. Although he would soon.

As he faced Leandra, she watched him with blank eyes. "Dey do not want me. I'm a killer, remember, Cross? Or are ya too...forgiving? The blood on my heart doesn't bother you?"

"It bothers you more than it will ever bother any other. The lives you claimed were evil ones. And your mistakes were made in ignorance, because tainted creatures warped your young mind." Her cat's eyes glowed as she struggled with something inside. "How long will you fight what you are?"

Leandra laughed, her eyes moving to meet Shadoe's. "I have no need t' fight anything. De Council doesn't want me, not one like me. They track the ones they want, Cross. Much like ya did with dis one," Leandra drawled.

Benjamin gave a low bark of laughter. "Darling, they are probably scared shitless of you," he suggested as he drew Shadoe to the bed, urging her to sit, resting his hands on her neck and rubbing with the balls of his thumbs.

Hmmm...did she realize she's naked? he wondered, grabbing a sheet and tucking it around her body, hiding it from sight—with regret.

Swinging back around, he listened politely as Leandra laughed mockingly.

"Some of dem, maybe. But I do not see fear stopping the majority." A cool, humorless smile curved her full wine-red painted lips as she said, "I am just another witch, after all. And not so impressive compared to dis one."

Finally, Shadoe's silence ended as she surged up off the bed, moving to stand with her back against an interior wall, as though being near the window disturbed her. She demanded, "Okay...now... I want to know what in the hell is going on?"

Evil lurks around us. Shaking her head, the thought faded away. He could hear her chaotic thoughts as he tried to find the words to explain what was going on.

But Leandra beat him to it.

"He's a Hunter. He kills all sorts of nasty creatures, like evil vampires, evil werewolves...evil witches," Leandra said calmly.

"And he preys on those who spill de blood of de innocent. So why haven't I died yet?"

Shadoe frowned. "You seem a little too eager to embrace death."

Leandra's lids flickered and she said quietly, "When you are left with de thoughts I live with, death sometimes seems a sweet release."

Benjamin's hands flexed, his jaw clenching as he stared at the exotic woman sitting there.

They were losing her. Leandra was sliding farther and farther into her self-imposed exile. Although she battled the darkness inside her, she would lose eventually, seeking out her death willingly. If they didn't stop it.

No. Damn it, no, he thought furiously as he glared at her. "If we wanted you dead, dead you would be, and you know that," Benjamin said flatly, drawing her gaze to him. "There's a difference between darkness and torment, and true evil. You have seen evil, Leandra. You are not it."

Something moved in her gaze, and for a moment, he glimpsed raw torment before her eyes closed and her head fell back, the wooden beads on her braids clacking together. A sigh lifted her breasts as she laced her hands on her flat belly. "I do know what I am, Hunter of de Council. I have no place in dis world."

Then her lashes lifted and she focused that uncanny stare on Shadoe. "But I am not de concern here now, am I? You have evil stalking all around you, girl," she said quietly, her nose wrinkling as she breathed in the stench of the cowering were. "He tastes evil. Feels evil. But it is through weakness. He sought more than he could ever hope to be, and landed here. Petty evil. You have a much larger one dat you must meet."

Shadoe shook her head. "I don't understand any of this. Damn it, yesterday things were *normal*." Her heart was rabbiting in her chest and she could hardly breathe around the thunder of it. The woman sitting across from her was a total stranger.

But she felt a kinship to her, something that made her feel this woman would understand the darkness inside her soul. The fear. The doubt.

Leandra laughed softly. "Your life stopped being normal ages ago. If it ever was. De magick inside you saw to dat." The musical lilt of her voice, rich with the islands, was oddly soothing, even as her eyes started to glow and swirl. "Open yourself to de magick, and it will guide ya better than any of us could ever hope to."

The tension in the air thickened as Leandra and Shadoe stared at each other. Building and building until the werewolf that Benjamin had secured in the hall started to howl and snarl.

"He's an uppity ting, isn't he?" Leandra drawled, rising from her sprawl on the chair and stalking over to the hall, peering at the werewolf who was bound hand and foot with reinforced cuffs.

"Bitch," the man snarled at her as the fear inside him tried to induce the change. His face was lengthening, slowly, as though he battled it. Fur was forming thicker and thicker on him.

Shadoe wrapped her arms around herself, rocking back and forth on her heels as she stared at him.

But he didn't pay any attention to Shadoe, his eyes rapt on Leandra's dark honey-gold skin. "Bitch. You walk with the Hunters but you bear one of our marks," he spat, his eyes focused on the small tattoo next to her eye.

Stroking it with one slender, red-tipped finger, Leandra purred, "Then ya should be more careful, stupid wolf. I do not fight fair, like dey do. My rules are not de same as deirs, so do not push me."

The spell Benjamin had wrapped around the werewolf splintered under the bastard's fear as he stared up into the eyes of death.

Shadoe swallowed, hearing the dry click in her throat just before the thick, wet popping sounds coming from the man drowned out all else. He bellowed, the enraged, painful shout changing to a long, echoing howl.

Leandra's eyes met Shadoe's.

Then the Jamaican looked at Benjamin and quietly said, "She really need to learn about de world dis way?"

Benjamin swore softly as he took in the pallor of Shadoe's face, the haunted look in her cornflower blue eyes. But when he moved to block the shifting werewolf from sight, she pushed him aside. "That is what Marcus is," she whispered thickly. "What Jimmy was. I really did see them changing."

"Yes," Benjamin said softly, moving to hold her against him, stroking her hair as she watched the change complete, her eyes stayed rapt on the tightly bound werewolf, his ankles and knees forced awkwardly behind his back, robbing him of the ability to move anything more than his head.

"And if I really saw them, then I really did burn Jimmy's heart to ash," she said, forcing out the words. "I am what you say, aren't I?"

Benjamin cuddled her closer to him as he said sadly, "Yes. You are."

"Ya will be more," Leandra said obliquely. Then she sulked, her full lower lip poking out just slightly. "Now I have to travel with him as a damn wolf. So much for doin' tings de easy way."

"Mebbe I'll change him back. Now dat is painful, I hear. Not a nice thing," she mused. Then she slid her gaze back to Ben, a sly look there as she smiled. "Of course...since I'm not a Hunter, I don't have to use a Hunter's ways, follow his rules... A nice person would let the bastard rest a while and change back on his own."

A quicksilver grin lit her face as she drawled, "But I'm not a nice person."

Chapter Four

Shadoe stared at the ball of heat and light that hovered over her head, panic in every line of her face. "Okay. I made it, but now how do I put it away?" she asked, fighting to keep her voice level.

Benjamin laughed. "Just let it go, sweet. It's easier than you think."

But she clung tenaciously to everything, including the magick, and it wouldn't die. "Relax," he ordered firmly, moving to stand behind her. "You don't have to control it. Just let it exist, and it will come to your call when you need it."

Just days had passed since her startling revelations—too much had changed. And she was expected to control this... *Ah, baby, not control. Let it exist...* The words were just there, in her mind.

Shadoe felt something inside her relax as the words reverberated through her. Not control.

Watching the golden orb, she couldn't help the smile on her face as it simply faded away. "That was easy," she said disbelieving. "How could it be so easy?"

"That is the way it is supposed to be. You and I are going to skip the basics and go straight to the important stuff. You need to learn and I'm going to do whatever it takes to teach you," he murmured from behind her.

His breath was warm on her neck and a hot shiver raced down her spine.

Her nipples tightened immediately and Shadoe's breath skittered to a halt in her throat, for a long second. Her skin heated and she could swear she scented her own need in the air.

"What else do I need to know?" she asked shakily, trying to focus again on the magick. Benjamin laughed easily, and she wanted to turn to him and wrap her arms around him, lose herself in him as the sound rolled over her like a caress.

"There's a lot to learn," he said. "A lot. The question is where to begin…"

* * * * *

Benjamin could smell her, the hot, spicy scent of aroused woman and it punched him in the gut like a fist. Why it had come, he didn't know, but damn it, the scent of her need in the air was driving him to distraction.

Cautiously, he laid his hands on her shoulders, waiting for her to move away, to throw his hands off. When instead, she leaned back against him, a hot, hungry moan left his lips and he lowered his mouth to her shoulder, gently raking the skin exposed by her tank top with sharp teeth.

She shuddered, the long slim length of her body falling back against his. Sliding his hands down the length of her arms, he moved his grip to her waist and eased her fully back against him. "You feel perfect against me," he murmured. "You smell like a dark autumn night, mysterious, wild, dangerous. And powerful. I want to taste it, taste you. All of you."

Shadoe gasped as he set his teeth on her neck with a quick, fast nip. "Will you let me?" Benjamin asked gruffly.

She didn't say yes.

But when she didn't say no, either, Benjamin slowly turned her in the circle of his arms and covered her mouth, cupping her chin with his hand and touching nothing else. Nibbling first at the seam of her lips, he listened to her shaky, trembling sigh, her racing heart, scented the rich, sweet taste of hungry woman growing stronger in the air.

Hunger tore through him as her hands lifted to clutch at his waist. With a gentle tightening of his fingers on her chin, he urged her lips open and pushed inside, groaning deep in his chest at her taste. Like her scent—mysterious, powerful—but still somehow so...sweet, innocent. With his tongue, he flirted with her mouth, her lips, rimming it before thrusting deep. Her mouth opened wide under his as she gasped and her hands slid up his torso to grip his shoulders, the bite of her nails into his skin sending sparks of flame down his spine.

Against his chest, he felt the firm, rounded pressure of her breasts, the hot stab of her nipples through her bra and shirt. Her rounded, soft belly cuddled against his cock as he slowly stepped closer to her body. Her head fell limply back as he released her lips, cruising his way down her neck, pausing to lick at the pulse throbbing there.

Her pulse slammed against her skin so hard, it was a wonder it didn't bruise her. Dallying at that soft, sweet spot, he licked, nuzzled, and caressed, then raked his teeth down her neck, feeling hot male pleasure course through him as she shuddered against him.

"You're sweet," he groaned against her skin, taking her hips in his hands and bringing her closer, pumping his cock against her, feeling hot satisfaction course through him when her knees buckled.

So damned sweet...he thought, desperate for more, for all.

Ben fell to his knees in front of her, still supporting her weight as he pressed his mouth to her belly, moving lower and lower until he could press his mouth against her mound through the layers of her clothes. Her body jerked and her hands fisted in his hair. Rolling his eyes upward, he met her gaze over the length of her body, seeing the dark storm building in her eyes, and the embarrassment. The curiosity...

Hooking his hands in the waist of her denim shorts, he tore them off, the heavy material shredding under his hands, the scraps falling to the ground. Taking one thigh from behind, he opened her and pressed his mouth against the damp cleft, tasting her through the lacy scrap of her panties, a hungry growl trickling from his lips at her sweetness.

"Damnation…I want more," he groaned.

"Ben," she gasped, tugging his head and staring at him.

"Shadoe…sweet, sweet Shadoe," he whispered. One jerk of his wrist tore the panties away, baring her from the waist down, and he tumbled her to the floor. Pushing her thighs wide, he stared down at her, the damp silk of her sex gleaming, her folds wet and open.

"What are you doing?" she shrieked, trying to close her thighs.

"Looking at you, getting ready to taste you," he answered, effortlessly keeping her from closing herself against him. Stroking one finger down the folds, he lifted it to his lips and added, "Teasing you."

"Don't look at me," she demanded, her face flushing, her eyes sparking with embarrassment.

"Have to, you're too pretty not to," he argued gently, smiling wickedly. Lowering his head, he pressed his mouth to her and feasted, driving through her folds, entering her, before moving higher and rasping his rough tongue over her clit, suckling the hard little bud deep.

A harsh, desperate moan left her and her eyes widened as she arched her hips against him, rocking feverishly. He pushed two fingers inside her tight, slick passage, pumping shallowly and listening to her whimper. *Damn me*, Benjamin thought wildly.

He hadn't ever wanted a woman this powerfully before, this quickly. His needs had fallen to the wayside next to his mission, the fire to find the child who had gone missing from his pack so many years ago. He had found her, and for the past five years, he had waited for her to leave the damned prison where they had sent her, fighting the urge to get her out, even if it involved tearing the place apart, stone by stone. *Dying* to tear the place apart stone by stone.

He'd waited patiently, unfaltering in his purpose, ignoring the needs of his body, ignoring his own hunger as he waited for her to be freed, so he could take care of her, bring her back home.

Ben hadn't expected to want her like this, hadn't known he *could* want like this.

Hell, he hadn't thought of wanting her at all, not until he had seen her walking down the street that first day, so lost, so confused, the wind blowing those long, deep brown curls around her heart-shaped face.

The wet, creamy heat of her pussy clamped around his fingers as she tumbled closer to climax. The tight, hot grip of her sheath started to milk his fingers rhythmically as she moved closer and closer. Those delicate tissues, those little muscles, and *damn it*, her scent…all of it combining and threatening to drive him mad.

She was close to coming. Ben could feel it in the tensing of her body, in the glazing of her eyes, her erratic, unsteady breathing.

"Perfect," he grunted against her, flicking his tongue across her clit. "Come…come, sweet, sexy Shadoe, come for me. Let me taste it."

At his words, she erupted, a flow of cream spilling from her, her sheath contracting around his fingers as Shadoe pumped her hips harder. Working herself up and down on his fingers, riding him as she screamed, a short, choked sound. He sucked on her clit, harder and harder, as she rode the wave of climax, her face flushed, her mouth trembling and swollen.

"Hmmm…that's good," he whispered in approval. "Good…" A violent shudder racked his body and he felt the hungry animal inside him straining at his chains, to fall and ravage this sweet little prize. Sucking in air, Benjamin lifted his eyes, staring at her over the length of her body as she too gasped for air.

Levering his body over hers, he let her feel the light brush as he whispered, "Shadoe, look at me."

Her eyes fluttered open, still dazed, still glowing with little sparks of untamed magick.

"Ben," she purred, arching her back unconsciously as she rode the orgasm through, pressing hot, hard little nipples against his chest, rubbing her mound against him.

"Sweet, ah, hell," he groaned. "Don't do that, sweet, unless you are ready for me to finish this."

A hungry look slid through her eyes, one that called to the animal in him, and she dug her nails into his shoulders. "Finish it, bet your ass you will," she murmured, licking her lips. Then a hot flush rushed to her cheeks, as though she couldn't believe she had said that.

Delighted, Benjamin grinned. "Oh, yeah. I'll finish it." Cupping the curve of her ass in his hands, he arched his hips against her, feeling the wet heat of her cream scalding him through his clothes.

It was amazing to feel that burning, driving heat from her, to see that punch of desire in her eyes. When before she had been so frightened by the mere scent of his lust. It was the wolf inside her, rousing. He could feel it. He damned the bastards who had given her cause to fear straight to hell, as he lowered his mouth to hers, teasingly, gently.

Pushing his tongue inside her mouth, he groaned at the taste of her and his balls drew tight against his body as his cock throbbed and pulsed for *her*. The need to drive his aching sex inside her sweet, wet pussy was nearly robbing him of thought, of control.

But she had to be ready—had to think of nothing but *this*. Nothing but the touch of his mouth on hers, his hands on her sweet, sexy little body, his cock sliding into the tight wet glove of her sheath. He couldn't take it if he saw that fear in hers eyes as he took her.

Shadoe rocked her hips up, shifting her legs to hook around his waist, parting the tender flesh between her thighs and cradling his denim-covered cock there. "Ummm...that feels so good," she gasped, her lids lowering until only a sliver of dark blue was visible as she stared at him. "So nice."

Benjamin grinned, albeit a little painfully. "We'll make it feel better, Shadoe, promise," he crooned against her lips, licking the full lower one and tugging on it with sharp, gentle teeth, shuddering when it had her arching against him.

Shifting to his knees, Benjamin tore his shirt away before shoving to his feet and tearing his jeans off, tossing them aside. The clink of loose change and keys sounded as his pockets emptied, and his jeans landed with a dull thud several feet away. A ripple rolled down his spine and he fumbled at the loss of control. He controlled the Wolf's power, damn it. So why did he suddenly feel so out of control?

Kneeling before her, Benjamin slowly removed the rest of her clothes, staring at the smooth, pale length of her body, the full, rounded weight of her breasts, topped with deep pink nipples. Her torso narrowed down to a slim waist, a full, female flare of hips, and short, curly wisps of hair covered her mound. Pearls of cream clung to her, dampening the hair, gleaming wetly under his stare. Her long, sleekly muscled thighs shifted restlessly as she stared up at him, her eyes clouded and hungry. "Benjamin, please," she whimpered, her long, tangled hair spread under her shoulders like a blanket.

"Oh, I'll please," he muttered, lowering his body over hers, licking her lips, diving inside her mouth while lower, his hands cupped her hips and lifted her against him. "I'll please you, baby. I swear it." Wedging her thighs apart, he angled his hips and started the first slow, deep thrust inside her. Sweat beaded on his brow and he gritted his teeth. "You're tight. Tighter than a virgin."

She mewled deep in her chest, thrashing her head back and forth, trying to draw him deeper. "I am a virgin, Ben...oh!" Her breath caught in her throat as she lifted her hips tentatively against him, trying to draw him deeper inside.

Benjamin stilled, locking his jaw. Bloody damn hell... Of course she was a virgin. The shy, private creature she had been before Jimmy wasn't likely to have indulged in wild sexual flings. And she had spent five long years in prison. Staring down at her, he felt his heart stutter in his chest. Pretty pink nipples stabbed up at him, the pale ivory of her skin flushed with excitement. The pulse in her throat throbbed beguilingly and her eyes were wide, dilated, locked on his face.

So damn sexy, so damn soft.

Pressing his forehead against hers, he whispered, "I'm keeping you," as he sank further inside her tight, wet pussy, the soft, silken hairs caressing his cock as he forged deep, through her slick, swollen tissues.

Her breath caught, and she stiffened against him, arching up as pain started to burn her pussy.

"Shhh...it's almost over," he crooned, nibbling at her neck, her chin, brushing his lips against hers. "Relax...open to me."

Shadoe's eyes burned with tears. Her pussy ached, burned, where before it had been throbbing with pleasure. Too deep, too hard, too much... She tried to pull her hips back but his big hands stopped her. "It hurts," she groaned, her head falling back as she sucked in air.

"It's your first time—I know it hurts...relax," he ordered gruffly, shifting his weight until suddenly he was rubbing against her clit, and Shadoe flinched at the hot little jolt of pleasure that arced through her. He did it again and again until she was lifting herself to each caress, eagerly, hungrily. That felt...oh...too much.

All of it was too much.

He took her mouth in a deep, drugging kiss and Shadoe sobbed against his lips as he circled his finger around one stiff, tight nipple. Taking his mouth from hers, he met her eyes. "Pretty," he whispered, holding her gaze as he pinched the hard little bud, plumping the soft flesh in his hand.

Her breath shuddered out of her lungs, and she lifted again for the slow stroke of his pelvis against her clit, the throbbing little mass of tissue swollen and aching. He slid deeper, and deeper, forging his way through her tight, slick tissues as she moved against him, seeking that brush of his body that made the ache in her belly draw tighter and tighter.

A startled, sharp cry left her as he sank completely into her, his pelvis pressed against her clit, sending hot sparking bolts of heat through her pussy, heating her belly, as she moved higher and harder against him until, with a sob, she climaxed around him.

Oh, she had come before. Self-pleasuring was a necessity inside prison, especially for one who wasn't interested in pursuing a relationship with another woman.

But that was nothing compared to this… It echoed and tore and burned its way through her until she was sobbing with the intensity of it. Heat built in her belly, scalding waves of it that pushed her farther and farther into a blinding maelstrom where she couldn't think, couldn't see, couldn't breathe without tasting Ben.

It even overshadowed that hot, glorious climax he had given her when he had gone down on her, lapping at her folds with long, thorough strokes of his tongue.

The muscles inside her pussy clung to his shaft as he pulled out and surged slowly back inside. When her eyes flew open at the stroke of his fingers on her clit, she could see him staring at her, his dark golden-brown eyes hooded, hungry, hot, almost a palpable touch as he watched her.

"Damn, you're pretty," he rasped, lowering his head to lick at her lips, nibble on the full lower one before he sought entrance to her mouth, driving inside with hungry motions that mimicked his hips against hers.

Her nails dug into the ridge of muscle along his shoulders as she lifted her hips to his, squeezing down with her muscles to hold him inside. A soft wail filled the room, and Shadoe couldn't believe that hungry, needy noise came from her.

Ben drove inside again, harder, as he shifted his weight to one elbow and reached down, sliding one hand over her torso, leaving a burning path of sensation as he arrowed in on her clit, circling it with firm, steady strokes of his thumb. The need to come again slammed her, drawing and coiling tight in her loins, a gnawing ache that demanded satisfaction. Shadoe buried her fingers in his hair, kissing him ravenously as she started to pump her hips to his, taking him deeper, harder, quicker and he let her, levering his weight off of her and letting her work herself upward against his cock.

The thick, burning pillar of flesh scalded her and Shadoe screamed when he dropped his weight and started to pound her with deep, driving thrusts of his cock inside her sheath, fucking her desperately as he plundered her mouth, his hands sliding under her, fingers curling over her shoulders to brace and hold her still for his thrusts. Just before the night exploded inside her, flooding her with hot, whirling jolts of electric, liquid heat, he climaxed inside her with a muffled roar.

Her lids drooped and darkness swarmed in front of her for a long, brief moment as she struggled to breathe, to pull herself back together. After a long, futile fight to get oriented, she gave up and cuddled against him, feeling his hands come up to hold her lovingly against him.

"Sweet, sweet Shadoe," he murmured.

The sound of her name on his lips serenaded her to sleep, and she basked in the comfort of finally feeling truly safe.

Chapter Five

When the wolves didn't return as expected, Marcus seethed. Blood flew and flesh was shredded as he took his fury out on Linus, the older, soft-spoken Alpha who had once lived quite happily in this town, taking the occasional runaway or drive-through tourist in an effort to satisfy the lust and the blood hunger inside him. Marcus' arrival had changed all of that and Linus catered to Marcus' every whim, albeit reluctantly.

Now the bloody, broken body of the Alpha lay in the corner and Linus suffered in silence as he waited for his body to heal enough for him to flee. Marcus Winston wasn't leaving this town to Linus, ever. The promise to move on had been empty. Something had drawn him here from the beginning and Marcus would stay.

Already, Linus knew one of the things that so obsessed Marcus, the girl, a dark-haired half-breed who didn't smell completely witch, completely wolven, but a sweet, hot scent that combined and seduced and beckoned any Alpha male to her.

No. Marcus wouldn't be leaving as long as the bitch was around. But the bitch was an even scarier thing than Marcus, and Linus clapped his teeth shut every time somebody so much as breathed a word about trying to get her. They'd all die. Plain and simple.

Death wasn't her angel, this girl. It didn't torment her every step, and she seemed at ease with herself, if not with life. But he wasn't laying a hand on that damn girl. Too many bad things lurked around her and protected her. Death lay in those around her.

He wasn't messing with them. No, not Linus.

As he breathed in, the pain coursed through him with agonizing intensity.

The skin on his back hung in bloody strips, and breathing was pure torture, with his broken nose and broken ribs. But each breath healed him a little more. So he forced himself to keep breathing, to block out the pain as best as he could, and just *breathe*. Like water evaporating, slowly each wound became less and less. Several hours after the beating, he had healed enough to shift. The werewolf magick would heal the rest of his wounds during the shift and then he could flee.

His pack had deserted him, craving the frequent blood that Marcus promised.

But Linus wasn't stupid.

The bloody rampages Marcus promised would bring one thing they didn't want, the attention of the Hunters. And Linus would be damned if they thought he would stand against the Hunters.

Bitter humor tore through him at that thought.

It wasn't possible to stand against the Hunters. A soft, pathetic whine left his mouth, animalistic sounding even though he still retained his human form. For now.

Gathering his strength, Linus focused and felt the change slide through him, agonizingly slow as the were magick forced his flesh back together and knit the broken bones. He was a whimpering, sopping wet pile of wolf flesh when it was over — exhausted, hungry, and desperate to flee.

Only a handful of his once proud clan remained. All clinging to Marcus.

Screw them, he thought angrily.

They could die with Marcus.

And they would. The girl… She wasn't what they thought. And the man with her —

Linus had seen the man who followed her, who watched her. His scent was everywhere she went. He guarded her.

The others were too blind to see it. Marcus, too arrogant.

Everything about him screamed Hunter.

Dragging himself to his feet, Linus swung his great, maned head left then right, listening, smelling… He was alone. Marcus had taken the females out, and the two betas remaining were most likely out chasing their tails. A great, heaving sigh left his powerful chest and Linus padded out of the room, his oversized timber wolf body making no sound.

He left through an open window, and didn't stop, not even once, to look back.

* * * * *

Marcus found the house empty.

The scent of blood and pain was thick in the air, but stale.

The little fucker had dared to leave. The women clung to Marcus, their eyes wide with shock, fear heavy in their scent. Nobody dared to disobey Marcus. But Linus had. He hadn't just disobeyed, he had *left*.

A furious snarl left him and he spun away from the women, the bitches. Two of them, only two left. And two good-for-nothing betas. They had next to no brains in their heads and even less power.

Should have pounded one of them—*no*, the blame for the failure went to Linus' shoulders. Even though he hadn't been with his wolves, he was their Alpha and should have trained them better.

But if he had beaten a beta, the Alpha, the only intelligent werewolf in the pathetic pack Marcus had taken over, would still be here.

The question was what to do about it.

If Linus had shifted before fleeing, and of course, he had, his injuries were all but a memory now and a night of feasting would give him the energy he needed to regain his strength.

Even if Marcus sent all four remaining werewolves after Linus, the Alpha would best them.

If Marcus went after him, wasting precious time, he'd leave the half-breed slut here alone. She needed watching.

No.

She needed breaking.

He was furious about the bastard sniffing at her tail. Who the hell did that shit think he was?

Nobody tried to touch what Marcus had claimed. He had marked that little piece of tail years ago and worse, she had *hurt* him. No mongrel bitch ever did that to him and got away with it.

She was going to bleed for that. And not just from a pitiful mark on her tit, either. Although he'd add to that one.

He'd rape her until she bled, beat her until she couldn't breathe for the screams, and then he would let her die. Slowly. Bleeding from a hundred different little nicks he'd put on that ivory hide.

She'd totally fucking rue the day she had dared not to cower before him.

Oh, yes. Jillian Morgan was going to suffer.

* * * * *

"Shadoe Wallace," she whispered, staring at her reflection.

"My name is Shadoe Wallace."

Jillian no longer felt like *her*. Jillian had lived in fear, in solitude for the past five years. Before that, she had been a wallflower, always on the outskirts, never one of the crowd. But now…

She was no longer the wallflower.

Staring at her reflection, nearly two weeks after Benjamin Cross had opened her eyes to *life*, Shadoe barely recognized herself.

She had taken a lover.

She walked down the streets with her head up, and no fear in her eyes.

Small sounds at night didn't send her into a panic attack.

She felt *free*.

It showed in her face, her bright, gleaming eyes. If she wasn't careful, they glowed. Her skin was clearer, brighter, a peaches and cream complexion she had never noticed before.

She glowed with health and vitality.

Shadoe Wallace.

Jillian Morgan was long gone.

And she liked who she saw staring at her from the mirror.

Lifting her hands, she cupped them in front of her face and breathed magick into them, the latest little power Benjamin had shown her. She could watch her entire life in her hands, from her birth, to now. And she could focus her thoughts on one person, somebody she knew, and be one with that person.

Leandra.

A guard at the prison who had befriended her.

A remembered favorite teacher.

Ben, that slow, sexy smile and the gold of his gleaming eyes... She sighed as his image shimmered into focus within her mind. *Mmmm...Ben...*

He was so amazing, so...*magickal*.

And he thought *she* was magick.

How amazing was that?

"This is a rare gift. I can focus on a person long enough to link with that person for short periods. You can actually merge with them, be one with them. Follow their thoughts back to birth, know their deepest secrets," he had whispered as his magick *hands*—some unseen touch of his—guided her through it.

"It's a responsibility," she murmured. One she couldn't abuse.

"Yes. It is. Not many understand that, and that's what makes you different, makes you more."

As she drifted now, she touched lightly on the minds of those she passed, never really intruding, just testing herself, refining the ability.

She'd need it desperately one day, she suspected.

A sudden jolt of terror filled her, a foul evil touch that locked her breath in her lungs, and turned her belly to ice.

A scent, one that she logically shouldn't be able to place, flooded her mind. It wasn't something she was actually smelling, in the here and now, but something *else*.

A scream filled her mind. Terrified, pain-filled, hideous.

Alone in her room, she pressed her hands to her temples and struggled to block it out, and her eyes fell on the mirror.

It was a good thing the terror had frozen her lungs.

Otherwise, she would have screamed. Pure bloody murder.

It wasn't her reflection she saw, wasn't her room in the mirror.

It was Marcus, the bastard who had tried so long ago to rape and kill her. She could see him, but only because he was standing next to a mirror as he lifted his hand, a hideous, leaded cat-o'-nine-tails held in his grip, and he brought it down on the back of a person.

Too bloodied, too broken for the sex to be easily determined, the person cowered and screamed and moaned under the lash of the evil whip.

Hands came up to grip her shoulders, but before she could whirl around, screaming and terrified, a soft, gentle growl of a voice whispered, "Shhh… It's a merging. A deep one. His fury opens his being up to you."

Ben's warm, protective presence at her back steadied her and she whispered, "How do I stop it?"

His voice was odd, questioning, when he asked, "Stop the merging? Is that what you really want? Or do you want to stop *him*?"

Shadoe couldn't stop the whimper in her throat any more than she could stop the shudder of fear that racked her. "Stop him? I *can't*. Don't you know what he did to me? What he could have done?"

His hands rubbed soothing circles on her shoulders and he said, "Yes. I know. But then, you didn't know what *you* could do."

His words ran through her, sending a frisson of something unrecognizable skittering down her spine. Heat sparked in her gut, unfurling and spreading through her before she even recognized it as anger. Wind blew around her, whipping her hair about her face as she continued to stare through the window of the mirror she was still bound to. Around one blood-streaked wrist, she saw a charm bracelet, silver, thin and delicate. Delicate, like the wrist.

He was beating a woman, beating her bloody.

And the way his mouth curved up at one corner, she knew he was enjoying it. Rage flooded her. Heat spilled through her, rolling like a river, building and building, but she didn't know how to focus it. Sending a pretty ball of visions wouldn't do shit against him. Her skin started to ache and she whimpered softly. "It hurts—" she choked out. "Why does it hurt?"

"You just don't know how to release it," Benjamin said slyly. "I do." He slid his hands from her shoulders to her hands as his power slid inside and mingled with hers, his psychic hands taking hers. "Watch."

He cupped her power. She could think of no other way to describe it. He cupped her power in her hands and forged a solid beam of magicked heat that he then urged her to focus on Marcus. "Now…you know what to do."

She opened the bowl of her hands, both psychic and physical. "I'd like to see you try it again, bastard," she whispered raggedly, unaware of the tears streaming down her face.

As Marcus lifted the whip to strike the helpless, bloodied girl again, Shadoe released it.

Her eyes could see little, just a ripple like the heat shimmering above pavement. But she could feel it inside as it burst from her, leaping toward Marcus, through the distance that separated them.

And she watched through the mirror as it struck him, knocking him off his feet, charring the front of his shirt with the heat of the power, sending him careening back into the wall behind him. Her gaze narrowed as it landed on the whip he still clutched. Cocking her head, she studied the whip. She wanted it wrapped around him, the leather biting into his skin, cutting him. A short, startled scream left her lips as the whip snaked up with a life of its own and wrapped around Marcus even as he swore and struggled against it. Big, powerful hands gripped the lashes and tried to keep it from him, but still it constricted, tighter and tighter.

"Sweet heaven," she whispered shakily. Behind her, she could feel Ben's approval as he wrapped his arms around her and hugged her tight.

Marcus was jerking against his bonds, swearing furiously, wrapped from shoulders to toe in leather. More leather than the whip had been made of, and still it continued to enshroud him, until from the shoulder down, he was wrapped in the leather and no skin showed, from the shoulders down.

"Fucking pathetic, sniveling little bastard—come out and face me," he snarled, the bones in his face rippling.

"He's trying to change," Benjamin said quietly. "Do you feel it coming on him?"

She could, but only distantly. The power was raw, primal. Alien, yet somehow familiar. Something inside her stirred, and frightened, Shadoe shoved it all away from her.

"I'll be damned…" Benjamin whispered.

The bones in Marcus' face, elongating, a muzzle forming, froze in mid-shift and they watched as it was absorbed back into his skin, sliding in like water.

"You stopped his shift. His power, I feel it, you displaced it somehow." The low, gravelly words were soft, awe-filled. She could feel his pleasure warming her like the sun.

"Who the fuck are you?" Marcus bellowed, and she watched as fear entered in his eyes.

Unable to stop herself, she moved forward, toward her mirror and reached out, laying her hand on it, feeling it ripple under her palm.

"Don't you know?" she asked coolly.

The jolt of his eyes struck her to the soles of her feet, but she refused to show the fear that bubbled inside her along with her rage.

"Forgotten me already? I never forgot you," she said flatly.

Benjamin couldn't stop the smirk that curved his lips as he stared at Marcus through the mirror, struggling against the leather bonds, and snarling furiously. Marcus could see them now.

"Fucking whore, stupid bitch," he spat, his eyes gleaming maniacally.

"Touch her again and I'll tear you apart," she whispered, ignoring him, not listening to the fear roiling in her gut. Her eyes went to the bloodied mess of the woman and her heart skittered.

She wasn't breathing anymore.

Marcus started to laugh. "Your threat is a little late, Jillian," he said in a singsong voice. "The little bitch's body was too weak. She's gone, chasing after her tail in the great beyond."

Benjamin's lips peeled back from his teeth and he snarled, feeling the rage tear through him, hot and powerful, primal. The Wolf inside him struggled against the bonds Benjamin slammed down, keeping the animal hidden. But his eyes still flickered and glowed, swirling with the rampant energy coursing through him.

"You're going to pay," Shadoe whispered raggedly. Her hands slipped from the mirror and she asked in a voice thick with tears, "I want him out of my head."

Cupping her face in his hands, Benjamin focused on the bond that merged Marcus to Shadoe. Through it, he could feel Marcus' torment of her as he jeered, "I'm going to *live* inside your head, fuck that mind that you opened to me. I'm gonna make you *suffer*, Jillian."

"My name is Shadoe," she rasped as her eyes met Benjamin's.

"Good girl," Benjamin murmured as he simply severed the link between them.

At the severing of the link, the strength seemed to evaporate from Shadoe and she stumbled against him, air burning in and out of her throat. "Good girl," Benjamin again whispered against her ear. "That's my Shadoe."

* * * * *

The leather was wound so tightly, biting deeply into his flesh that Marcus couldn't get the leverage he needed to tear it. Shifting would have done it, the larger mass of the wolf simply shredding the leather as it exploded out of his human form.

But she had done something.

Blocked the animal inside.

"You are the animal…" a soft, disgusted voice said. It was a familiar voice, one that Marcus either ignored or abused, depending on his mood.

"Shut up, you old dog," he spat at the Wolf. Try as he might, he couldn't rid himself of that righteous, powerful creature, the creature his shifter abilities had come from.

"Oh, you could rid yourself of me. Find a silver bullet," the Wolf taunted nastily.

"You shouldn't want me so easily dead—if I die, you die," Marcus growled, struggling to find the path that would lead to the Wolf's power and let him shift and tear free of the leather binding. How could there be so much? The lashes of the cat had been less than eight feet long. He had so much leather hugging him, he could hardly breathe, and his body was growing slick with sweat.

The soft chuffing sound of the Wolf's laughter filled him and the Wolf said, *"If only you knew how wrong you are. If only you had learned as much of me as I have learned from you. I cannot die. I simply am. So I can wish for the end of your pathetic life and stay alive and well. Just more of a sinner."*

Marcus had the impression of something big and wolf-like studying him as he lay struggling, so he snarled, "Stop fucking watching me! Give me the wolf back. She stopped me from changing…or was it *you*?" Marcus cocked his head and hissed, "It is you…the little bitch couldn't. You did something."

More chuffing, and the Wolf's laughter echoed in his mind once more. *"You are such a stupid thing. How did my power land inside you? Not only does she have the power to do this, she has the power to destroy you, to lock the wolf's power out completely, forever, and you will go slowly mad inside, losing the ability to think, to see, to live."*

Marcus struggled within his leather cocoon as he shouted out in fury, "Give him back."

The Wolf laughed dryly. *"I did not take him. And truly, neither did she. She just…split the two of you. You'll have to find a way to get him back yourself."*

Then there was total silence as the Wolf withdrew, ignoring all of Marcus' demands and furious cursing.

The fury inside his gut ate a burning hole in it as he threw back his head and roared.

Of course, none alive were there to hear him. The Alpha had retreated, pulling back from his clan. The betas hid or chased the bitches.

Well, just one bitch to chase now. The other lay dead just inches from him. The one who could have freed him, he sulked. Stupid whore. If she had just done what she was supposed to—

Not that Marcus really knew what she could have done to lessen his rage.

The last bitch was probably pressed between the two betas, when they should have been watching Jillian. With a last, furious jerk, he stopped fighting and lay there.

Stewing, fuming, his anger roiling inside him.

* * * * *

When Sam finally finished cutting through the leather binding him, she scurried away on her hands and knees, her shoulder-length hair spilling around her shoulders as she trembled with fear.

She should have stayed with Linus. *Stupid, stupid bitch...always running your mouth*, she thought furiously, lowering her head and waiting for the beating to start.

"Get up, you little cunt," he snarled, striding by her. He had resolved not to kill this one. He needed the remaining wolves as extra eyes.

And fodder.

Just in case the Wolf hadn't lied.

And until he had Jillian cowering under him, for good this time, he needed the wolf bitch around. He didn't fancy going without pussy indefinitely.

Sam couldn't stop the surprised gasp that left her, but she sure as hell didn't stay huddled on the floor. If he changed his mind, she could run faster if she was already on her feet.

Chapter Six

Linus didn't like the way the woman looked at him.

Her amber eyes, almond-shaped, exotic and cool, narrowed on his face. Behind her, Jude was held motionless, his eyes half-empty, his body sitting limply in the chair.

If it wasn't for the occasional rise and fall of his chest, Linus would have thought his former second was dead.

How in the fuck had he managed to end up under the eyes of a Hunter? He had been fleeing just that situation, where had he captured their interest? They'd see the blood on his soul, the thirst for more that filled him.

"Well, now… What have we here?" the tall, lean witch asked, her eyes narrowed, her husky, softly accented voice stroking down his spine like silk dipped in poison. Deadly.

She was deadly.

"My man dere, he has your stink on his skin," she mused, lowering the cup she had been drinking black tea from. "I oughta know, I've been smelling dat foul stench for two weeks now."

She cocked her head, thick black braids falling over one shoulder as she studied him. "Ya know him. I saw dat in your eyes when you walked in here. Ya didn't run, though. I have to wonder why."

Linus sighed, shoving a hand through his hair. "Would it have done any good? You can't run from a Hunter. They will find you. You have to hope to not be noticed by them, witch."

He lowered himself into the seat across from her and waited with a cocked brow. At least death from a Hunter would be quick, and more merciful than anything Marcus could offer.

Two weeks away from him, and still Linus wondered if the bastard was going to come after him.

The woman laughed, the husky sound falling from her lips without amusement. "I be no Hunter," she said, shaking her head. The wooden beads on the end of her braids clacked together as she leaned forward. "Da Hunters, dey don't want one like me. My heart has almost as much blood on it as yours, ya sorry wolf."

His brow pinched and he shook his graying head. "I've never seen anybody more clearly a Hunter. And I've hidden from a lot. What trick is this?"

"No trick, mon," she said, shrugging. Under the black straps of the camisole she wore with her jeans, her shoulders gleamed a soft mellow gold, rounded, firm with muscle. "I am no Hunter. Dat is simple truth."

"Then what are you doing with him? He a date?" Linus asked sarcastically, sliding his gaze to his ex-pack mate. "He needs to liven up some, but since I know him, I know this isn't his normal behavior. I'd say he is drugged. Or bespelled."

"Oh, he definitely is not a lively boy," she chuckled. "Not since he tried to lay his filthy hands on me once we left Cross and his new lady. He thought dat a lone witch was weak. Eh, he is a man, of course. I could forgive his stupidity." She smirked. "I just chose to take offense instead. He's bespelled, all right. Chasing his tail, caught in de maze of his own mind. So now, he is like a baby, and I must lead him everywhere we go. No wonder it is taking so damned long."

"Why do I not think you are just being figurative?" Linus murmured, tugging on his short, iron gray goatee, stroking his mustache.

"Mebbe because ya be a bit smarter den he is," she suggested.

"Smart... If I was smart, I would have taken off running the minute that bastard stepped foot into my town. I thought I could wait it out, that he'd get bored and leave. But he wants the little witch," Linus murmured, rubbing his hands over his face, lifting tired eyes to study the menu painted on the wall. *One last meal…in a hole in the wall diner.*

Cocking a winged brow, she asked, "What witch?"

"Her name is Jillian Morgan. She just got out of jail for killing a man—self-defense, plain and simple, but they put her away for six years in the next town over," he said. "Some college punk, a werewolf that I ignored for the most part, attacked her in Buxley. I knew him, vaguely. Knew the wolf that bit him. And I remember reading about the mess in the paper. He was an infected wolf, not a born one, and young, stupid. When he tried to rape her, she killed him. She moved here once she got out of jail, on the outskirts of town. Looking for peace, I imagine. She won't find it there. Not with Marcus around."

The witch stilled, cocking her head. "Marcus…"

"Have you been unlucky enough to make his acquaintance?"

"No. No, I haven't—but his name, it stills something inside of me. De Council… I have an urge to share his name with dem," she said, her voice wry. "Just the sound of one man's first name. Why does it stir me so?"

"They say the Hunters know prey simply by a name, a voice, a whisper of his evil deeds," Linus said quietly. "Are you sure you are no Hunter?"

She smiled, a tiny, evil curve of her lips that chilled Linus to the bone. "If I were a Hunter, den ya'd be dead. Ya have much blood staining you—I can feel it. So aren't ya glad I'm no Hunter?"

"You aren't planning on killing me?" Linus asked warily.

"I'm not fit to judge another's sins, to cast judgment on another man for his crimes," she said quietly. "If ya can keep your hands clean, dey just might let ya live when ya do meet up wit' a real Hunter."

She rose, and like a puppet on strings, Jude followed, his motions short and jerky.

Linus sat there, staring at their backs, not even hearing the waitress as she finally approached the table.

In a soundless whisper, he murmured, "I've never known a truer Hunter."

* * * * *

Malachi pushed away from the table where he had been cuddling a plump, sweet-faced witch. Only her face was sweet, though; the raw power of witch that ran through her veins was heated, spicy, that of a warrior.

The door was still swinging on its hinges as Leandra strode in, her eyes glinting with purpose, her head held high. *Hmmm...not so broken now, are ye, sweet?* Mal mused as Casey drew her legs up to her chest and rested her chin on them, studying Leandra curiously.

Behind her, a man walked—forced, stuttering steps, eyes half-dead, a dumb look on his features. A spell. Mal could feel it, and under the purity of the spell, the man's foul, evil soul lived, cursing the bitch who had locked him in his own body.

"Takin' up Huntin', have ye?" Mal drawled, moving across the rich Persian carpet to meet her. His large bare feet were soundless, his hair spilling around his shoulders, a gentle smile on his face.

Leandra met his eyes squarely, cocking a black brow, an amused smile on her full, wine-red lips. "Ya joke, right? Me, a Hunter? My bloody soul staining the beauty of such a legacy?" She laughed.

Reaching out, Mal took her hand and lifted it to his lips. "Ye have the purest of souls, milady. Just so full of heartbreak, it almost hurts to stand so close," he murmured.

A minute shudder ran through her at his touch and for a moment, her eyes gleamed hot with lust. But just for a moment, because Mal felt the distinct lock of shields between them.

Cutting herself off from him, and weakening the effects of the vampire's call. With a wry grin, he said, "Have ya been talkin' to Kelsey, pretty witch?"

"Save your charms for somebody who wants dem, Malachi. I prefer to do me own choosin' when I take a lover. Not let my body choose," she drawled, gently tugging her hand away. "Now, would ya be so kind as to take this nasty ting away from me? His thoughts, dey are so foul, so dirty."

"Drop the spell from him, let him speak," Malachi said with a sigh, moving his eyes from the witch to the weakling at her side.

"As soon as I take de spell away, he is gonna try t' get his hands on me," she said, turning to study the drooling, slack-jawed wreck that followed her. "I can feel his thoughts, his mind, it works perfectly fine. And it is a nasty ting."

"Are you afraid you can't handle yourself against him?" Casey called out from the table. "He's just a sorry werewolf, no honor, no true power. A beta who thought he could be Alpha. He stinks with it, the blood of the innocent."

Casting Casey a bored glance, she said, "De day I can't fight a pathetic whelp like him is de day your Council starts taking in strays like him off de streets. Don't be tiresome."

The spell holding Jude dissolved and he lunged for Leandra, the rage fueling the change inside him and he was wolven by the time he reached her, swiping with one clawed hand to rip her throat out.

Leandra sprung away, drawing the dagger at her hip as she wagged her finger at him. "Now… What did I tell ya, mon? Try to touch me again and I'll see ya dead."

"Little cunt, you had me drooling like a damn retard," he snarled.

"Ach, now that's an ugly word… Nobody likes to be called a retard," Malachi said, shaking his head from his perch by Casey. "It's not very PC."

Behind him, Casey giggled. "You sound like the kids here, Mal. PC. Are ya going to start writing little notes with LOL and C-ya on them?"

He smirked, lifting one broad shoulder negligently as he studied Leandra at work.

She was behind Jude now, having him spinning like a top as he tried to catch her. With the light of battle in her eyes, she struck out, the silver knife sliding through his hide like butter. Hot blood spilled, striking the floor, running in rivulets down his side. "Silver, mon. Ya know how long it takes to heal a silver-wrought wound, wolf?"

He roared and lashed out, catching her in the face. She flew back, blood trickling from her lip. Flying into the wall, she hit and slid down, but had barely touched the floor before she rose to her feet, wiping the blood away and tossing her head back.

"Do ya know how I had to learn to fight? It was against bastards like you," she purred, stalking closer. "And they suffered and bled far more than I by de time I was done."

She dove forward, tucking her body into a somersault along the floor, coming up tangled under his feet as he tried to reach for her. With a nasty laugh, she plunged her knife upward, into his unprotected balls, twisting the knife and jerking it up before pulling out and rolling away from the flow of blood.

Malachi winced and muttered, "Ouch."

Casey whispered, "I wonder if she can teach me that little maneuver."

Smug, female laughter filled the room as Leandra rose, tossing her black braids over her shoulder. "I told ya, Jude, didn't I? Mebbe ya didn't tink I was serious," she mused, shaking her head. Gesturing to him with her knife, she tsked and said in a mournful voice, "Ya see de error of your ways, now don't ya?"

The wolf rose from his crouched position and in one final desperate lunge, he attacked.

Malachi stiffened as Leandra went down under the wolf, the sound of powerful teeth clacking together a final sounding echo in the room. Rising, he was at her side in an instant, grabbing the wolf by the scruff of his neck, digging his hand into muscle and bone as he threw him away.

Only to realize he was already dead, the fur receding and melting away into human form, the knife buried to the hilt in his chest. Piercing his heart.

Leandra lay there, a brow cocked up at him. "Honestly, now... Did ya think I'd die so easily, Hunter?"

He took her hand and pulled her to her feet, shaking his head in amazement. "A warrior, ye are quite the warrior, Leandra. Don't ye think it's time ya stop hiding from ye fate and join us?"

* * * * *

Malachi frowned darkly into the night as Leandra spoke, telling them about the witch who had been locked away for protecting herself. If they had found her, none of this would have happened.

"He calls her Shadoe?" Mal asked, casting Leandra a questioning look.

"Ya, he does. I found her real name before I left de town. It's Jillian Morgan. She was released from prison just a few weeks ago." A snarl curled her full, red lips and she said, "When dat pathetic wolf tried to attack her, Cross took care of him. But she took care of another. Never been trained, hardly even knows what she is, but she took care of herself. Dat Marcus, he wants her."

"I imagine he would," Malachi murmured. "His kind prey on the weak, the untrained, the young."

"She is not weak," Leandra said, frowning. "Untrained...and her magick, it smells *fresh*, like she has never used it before. But she is not weak. Very frightened, now she is dat."

"Benjamin Cross has been searching for years to locate a woman who was spirited away from his pack when he was but a boy," Malachi said softly. "Right when the murders started to happen. Some zealots who thought the Inherents and the werewolves should run wild and feed on humans tried to overtake the pack. They lived in a blended pack, both were and Inherent. Many good shifters died. The girl simply disappeared when they went to find her. She was gone, like she had never been there. Her mother was a witch—it's said she magicked the girl away, and none could find a trail to follow. Ben's father was killed as well, but the Council had learned of the murders and sent the Hunters in. We got there that night, the night they killed Ben's da. Ben was just a little thing, maybe five years old, and they had him locked up like an animal, using him to try and draw others out, so they could kill the *non-believers*, as they called the saner folks."

Leandra was silent, listening to him, her arms wrapped protectively around her body.

"He was just a baby," Malachi murmured, looking down at his hands, flexing them. He had enjoyed the blood he spilled that night, far too much. As one of the witches whisked Benjamin away, soothing and shushing his panicked crying for his mama and daddy. "Just a baby. They had him locked in a cage, for pity's sake."

"You tink he has found de girl dat went missin'?" Leandra asked, gently guiding the conversation away from memories of a boy caged like an animal.

"He's been searching for her for years. Another witch swore the child was vital to our fight. It may well be Carrick Wallace's child. If she is, she'll have the blood of Inherent wolf as well as witch inside her. She'd be a tasty treat for our enemies if they find her," Malachi said, heaving out a sigh, shoving thoughts of a broken boy out of his mind.

"Isn't dat what Cross is 'round for? To protect her and keep dem away?"

"Benjamin is a powerful bastard, not just Inherent, but with magick as well. But he cannot fight an army alone." Malachi wondered about the girl, wondering if hers was the faint scent he could catch on Leandra's skin from time to time. It was…unique. Not quite as tempting as Tori's. But never had he known a scent as tantalizing as the blood of the Huntress.

Running his tongue over his teeth, he wondered at this new witch's scent. How would she taste? Feel?

Chapter Seven

Her taste was divine.

It had been close to a week since Leandra had left them, since Shadoe had knocked Marcus on his ass and tied him with his own whip, all without even being in the room with him.

More than a week since he had first buried his aching cock in her sweet body, and Benjamin was quite certain he'd never have enough of her. Pushing his tongue deep inside her cleft, he growled against her, the demon of lust on his back riding him harder and harder.

She screamed out in climax, her fingers tangling in his hair as she arched, moving her hips up, riding his mouth. Her pussy convulsed around his tongue and while the orgasm was still tearing through her, he moved up on her body and drove his cock deep inside her drenched sheath. Shuddering in ecstasy as her rhythmic clenching around his cock stroked him and milked him, he clenched his teeth against the urge to come.

This sweet, hot little witch… He'd never have enough of her.

* * * * *

Hours later, he rose from the bed, the moon high overhead and mocking him.

She still didn't fully know what he was. Not completely. He had never shifted in her presence, and the need to shift, to hunt, was becoming strong. He could go a long time without shifting, but weeks? It was almost six weeks since he had run the night as a wolf, since he had last hunted. And the need to do so was driving him mad.

He feared her reaction, though.

She needed to know — had to. The beast that lurked within him dwelled inside her as well. She needed to know, and come to grips with what she was.

But her fear…

Sweat was forming thin and fine on his body. Moving out of the room, he left his clothes scattered on the floor, and Shadoe sleeping deeply on that bed.

He moved into the backyard, the full moon streaming brightly on his naked flesh. His skin rippled. Power flowed.

He sank to his knees, welcoming the rush as fur flowed and bones shifted and reformed. When he lifted his head, he was wolven, a giant timber wolf crouching low to the ground, then he took off running, bounding over the grassy lawn, and into the forest.

The scent of a deer, hot and rich with life, flooded his senses and he took off after the buck, hunger driving him on.

* * * * *

Malachi watched from the roof as Cross shifted. It was a smooth change, almost magickal, silent, full of none of the hideous sounds of breaking bones that normally accompanied a shifter's change.

He was hungry, that wolf was.

Nearly mad with the need to hunt.

But it didn't stop him from protecting the witch within the house. Malachi felt the shimmer of a spell settle over him, inspect him and accept him as Benjamin ran away.

He didn't try a spell as touchy as keeping everything out — that would have been a waste of time, as it would have sounded alarms as the defensive mechanism of the spell attacked every bug and bird that flew in. No, Benjamin set a web around the house, something that would withhold anything evil, and cling to it.

Of course, it didn't alert Benjamin to Mal's presence. Because Mal wasn't evil.

A bit of a deviant. But not evil.

Damned good witch, Malachi thought with approval. The Council had few of his ilk, both witch and other. The witchcraft many times cancelled out the other, nullifying the infection that came with the werewolf's bite. When bitten by a vamp, many times the bite simply killed the poor witch in question when her sire tried to bring her over as a vampire. Often enough, Hunters of the Council wed, mated and had a child, but the babe was often born without any abilities at all—the werewolf or Inherent genes canceling out the witchcraft, and resulting in a human child. Well, almost human... The children of such matings were nearly as long-lived as their parents.

The woman inside the house would be another. Malachi could scent it on her even from here, full of power, the pure, brilliant energy of witch, and the hot, pulsating power of wolf. He leaped from the roof, turning as he jumped and landing in a crouch facing the house.

Drawing in a deep breath, he felt his fangs start to swell and throb in their sockets. Enticing scent... What was it about the witches lately? Sweet, sweet Lori had drawn him terribly, and Kelsey—

He scowled when he thought of her. Damned contrary bitch, and then he had to deal with his own self disgust for calling her such. She was not a bitch, exactly.

She just...

Doesn't want me...

And that made her so much more intriguing. And she had been intriguing enough, tempting enough, before. She didn't need anything added to make her even more tantalizing. Especially since the woman in question tended to ignore him, completely and totally.

Her sweet, soft body, the coppery-red hair, and her eyes, those eyes that watched Malachi as though she knew him clear through his soul. His cock ached and hardened even thinking of her, his jaded libido rearing its head.

Kelsey…

A soft, hungry growl rose in his throat as he thought of her and frustrated, he shoved the thoughts to the back of his mind. Tempting…too tempting.

He'd think of nothing but her if parts of him had their way.

Striding to the back door, he laid a hand on it, absorbing the simple spell that had been placed there much earlier, the simple hearth binding that so many people unwittingly put on their lands over time as they made a home. Absorbing it, and letting his form shift slightly, just slightly, so that the spell didn't see him as a vampire, or as any sort of threat. As the spell tingled over him, he stepped inside.

He had gotten into many houses this way. The hearth binding spell was a simple but powerful one, the one that kept vampires out. Most vampires. As a human lived on one piece of land for a time, his essence started to mark it, stain it, permeate it, forming a barrier between the undead and the living. That's what it was…the house was that of the living, and it rejected those who weren't full of life. The owner of the land had to accept the undead before the land would. Very little hocus-pocus involved, and all of it unconscious.

Nothing so difficult had been done here and Malachi entered the house easily, wandering around, studying the house. There was little to study, outside of a small office.

She left no marks of herself in this house, nothing that shouted to the world…*this is mine!* Outside of the office that is. The office was most clearly marked, a few prints of faeries on the walls, tons of books, many of them ancient tomes she had no business owning.

But he could feel Benjamin Cross' mark on it. He had given these books to her, but it had been some time ago. Her mark was stronger than his now.

He felt her wake and he paused, wondering if he should… *Shit.*

"Who in the hell is in my house?" a low, angry voice demanded.

Anger, fury, and indignation. This was definitely a woman who was tired of being trifled with.

She had felt him. And worse…a distinct snick settled over the house, a locking spell, binding him in.

How the bloody hell had a new witch learned that so damned fast?

At the sound of her feet on the stairs, soft, silent, and certain, Malachi shifted to mist and hovered. No bloody way he was taking a chance at scaring her. The Good Lord above only knew how she would react and it might not be pretty.

If she was already managing a locking spell that entrapped a vampire, certainly she could manage fire. And he doubted she'd merely torment him with it, like Kelsey and the diabolical Leandra so enjoyed doing.

Testing, he tried one of the few unvampire-like skills to slip out from under the spell, but it didn't work. *Bloody hell*, Mal mused, settling in a corner, hovering in the darkness and waiting. She came around the corner, her bright blue eyes snapping with fire, full of rage and nerves and power. A dangerous combination.

A rather dangerous package, he mused, feeling something inside him stir as he shifted his insubstantial gaze from her eyes, down to a kissably soft mouth, the full lower lip making him pause — a very fuckable mouth, he thought.

Hmmm… His gaze rested there for a very long moment and his lust started to heat. Too fucking bad he could smell Cross all over her.

Her slender swan-like neck was left bare by the messy knot she had piled her hair into, loose tendrils corkscrewing all over strong, proud shoulders. Her breasts rose full and firm against the simple cotton of the button-down she wore, the darker shadow of her nipples catching his gaze next. Her softly rounded tummy and sleekly curved hips showcased that she was a woman, not some skinny stick who had a body harder than his. Long, slim, tautly muscled thighs were bare under the hem of the man's button-down.

Hmmm…delicious, he decided, slowly moving his gaze back up to her face. He heard the wolf bounding back, running on swift feet through the woods. The magick had called to him. Benjamin had felt Shadoe's magick and given up on his hunt, determined to get back to her side.

It was only moments before Malachi sensed the energy burst that came with a shape-shifter's return to his mortal skin. That was closely followed by the door blowing open, as targeted magick filled the room, seeking out Malachi, hovering below him.

"Shadoe? Go upstairs, I'll take care of this."

Malachi chuckled, letting the sound echo through the room. Benjamin started, looking around him, and then his eyes closed. "Your arrogance grows constantly, old man." When Ben's eyes opened, they were glowing, backlit with a gleaming golden hue.

His gaze flew to Malachi, locking onto his invisible form. Benjamin cocked his head and asked, "Are you going to show yourself, Mal? Or can I have the pleasure of making you?"

Malachi was still laughing when he reformed, holding a hand up in peace offering. "Honestly, Benjamin, if I didn't know better, I'd think that was a challenge," he said, grinning rakishly at Shadoe as she narrowed her eyes.

"You know this bastard that broke into my house?" she demanded, jabbing a thumb in Mal's direction. "And what in the hell are you doing walking around outside naked? This nudist streak of yours is getting disturbing."

"Nudist streak?" Mal questioned, but she barely even glanced at him before turning her angry eyes back to Benjamin.

"Yes, I know him," Benjamin answered flatly, staring at Mal with a dark, unreadable gaze. He conveniently didn't respond to the second half of her comment.

Mal could usually read a man easily, but Benjamin was—unique. Nothing about Benjamin Cross was as it should be, not his reactions, not his attitude, not his methods or his madness, Mal thought with a smirk as he kept his eyes on Shadoe. She was the unknown here, though, and the inexperienced. An inexperienced witch was often the most deadly. They simply didn't know what they could do.

"Then maybe you could tell me why the hell he is here?" the woman demanded.

Mal quirked a brow and before Benjamin could answer, he offered, "Ye could ask me yourself, pet. Did that occur to ye?"

Through gritted teeth, she answered, "But that would mean acknowledging you. I don't care to talk to you."

A frown darkened his face and Malachi had to bite his tongue to keep from snarling back at her. *A man breaks into her house, what do you expect?*

Well, maybe some of the female appreciation he was so used to would be nice. Even if it did grow tiresome from time to time, at least he wasn't facing such a sharp tongue from those ladies. Yes, there was a much softer side of her tongue he'd rather deal with, preferably as it laved the skin of his cock. Her scent was sweet, young, full of power and life.

"Malachi, would you care to tell me why you are here?" Benjamin asked, biting the inside of his cheek to keep from smiling. Yet another witch who wasn't too keen on the idea of falling to her knees to worship slavishly at the ancient one's feet. Or his cock.

Malachi was too used to that, and entirely too bored from it. And he didn't quite know how to handle a woman who didn't react in the normal way. From the arrogant tilt of his chin and the cool look in those blue eyes, Benjamin surmised that again he was left floundering by this reaction, and totally intrigued, if the way he was watching Shadoe was any clue.

Every protective, possessive instinct in Benjamin rose to the fore and he moved toward Shadoe, resting a hand on her hip and drawing her closer. She slid him an odd look, but didn't move away.

Mal tracked the move and as Benjamin met the ancient one's eyes, Malachi smiled, a slow, sardonic curl of his lips. Then he replied, "According to Leandra, there is a man who is rather interested in you, Miss Wallace. Something about his name sat uneasily with a number of my compatriots. I'm here at their request."

That caught Shadoe's attention. Benjamin bit back the snarl that bubbled in his throat. *Your own damn fault*, he told himself. *Only yours.* He should have told her sooner. Much sooner.

"Compatriots," Shadoe said flatly. "Exactly who are these compatriots?"

Yet again, her world had shifted on its axis.

* * * * *

As Benjamin's words sank in, she sat silently on the couch, her arms wrapped around her legs.

A Hunter.

The Hunter's Council. Words Leandra had used, but Shadoe somehow had just not latched onto. Of course, she had been latching onto a little too much at the time. Like magick, and the fact that werewolves really existed.

Benjamin belonged to this nebulous Council.

And he had come searching for her. A Hunter who fought monsters like Marcus, Benjamin Cross had been seeking her for years before he'd finally found her when the trial had splattered her face, however briefly, on national news. And why had he been seeking her? Because this Council he said he belonged to thought she would be of use to them.

Wanted her to join them.

And her father...he had been one of them, before he met her mother. He had begged for release from the Council, wanting to live a normal life with his bride, to raise children and watch his family without fear that the monsters he Hunted would one day turn and hunt him.

The monsters had come, all right, but from his own people, not from the evil he had feared.

Her father… She could barely remember him, even now. A big booming voice, strong, wide hands, but so gentle.

Benjamin had been looking for her for a reason, she accepted that. But there was more to it than what she had thought. Much more.

"What else aren't you telling me?" she asked, her voice ragged and rough. "There's more, I know it."

Benjamin's eyes flicked to the silent, red-haired giant and she felt the air ripple as some silent communication flowed between them. The man Benjamin called Malachi inclined his head and leaned back against the wall, folding his arms over his chest, and waiting.

"We aren't human," Benjamin said without preamble.

Her eyelids flickered. "You look pretty damn human to me. Just because you can do magick doesn't make you nonhuman," Shadoe said, as a hard little knot of fear started to form in her belly.

"It's not just the magick," Benjamin said wearily, reaching up and rubbing his face. "There's so much more."

Her eyes moved to Malachi. "Are you human?" she asked warily, unwilling to ask what the "*more*" was.

He flashed a toothy, brilliant smile. "I was. Once. It's been so long ago, I scarcely remember it," he said, lifting one shoulder in a shrug.

She fell silent. She wanted to laugh at him, at them both. Laugh hysterically, because that had to be better than the slimy knot of fear that was forming inside her belly.

It had to be…

"Don't you want to know what I am?" Benjamin whispered, moving closer, slowly, gracefully, his eyes locked on hers. "What we are?"

When his hands came up and cupped her face, her skin heated, and she could feel herself shaking. As he brushed his lips against her cheek, he murmured, "You are safe with me, always."

Another telling look passed between Benjamin and the silent Malachi, and then Shadoe jolted as Benjamin's complete attention focused on her.

"I won't hurt you, ever… I want you to remember that," he murmured and then he stepped back.

She jumped when a rough growl trickled from his throat as he buried his face in his hands. Dizzying little streaks of pure terror flooded her belly as some wild energy filled the air around him. Fur was sprouting on those long, gentle hands that had loved her so thoroughly, touched and stroked every last inch of her body.

"Ben?" The word wobbled, full of fear. Shadoe didn't want to admit that voice was hers—so small and scared sounding. His hands fell away and she flinched when he met her gaze, through glowing, gleaming eyes as smooth, dusky skin melted away inside him, under the flow of fur—short, thick black fur that covered his entire body within moments. It was a soundless thing, even as his body jerked suddenly, and she muffled a tiny scream. She realized the bones inside his body were breaking to reform, elongating his arms and legs, changing his sleek body into a walking powerhouse of black fur and gleaming golden eyes.

It was smooth, so much quicker than Marcus' change had been while she fought him, almost eerily beautiful.

And she was so damned scared, she couldn't speak. There was a dry click in her throat when she swallowed, and her heart raced so damned fast and hard, it practically hurt.

Unaware she was even doing so, she backed away, shaking her head. *Nononononono*. The word echoed inside her mind, chasing itself around until it was all but vibrating inside her, growing louder and louder until it tore from her mouth in a scream.

"Shadoe, you are safe."

The words flooded her mind, almost overpowering her. She had been moving for the door, sidling along the wall when Malachi appeared in front of her — *poof*, like magick — he moved so fast. He caught her shoulders, then her face in his hands.

"He is no danger to *you*, Shadoe," the other man crooned, in a soft, accented voice that rolled over her like wet velvet, clinging, soft, stroking.

But memories too damned strong to fight refused to let her hear. Tearing away from him she ran, bolting out the door and running into the trees that bordered her house. *Nonononono*. This wasn't happening, couldn't be happening. It just wasn't possible.

Branches tore at her face, scratching her, jabbing her, tripping her. The moon had risen, a lovely half crescent that provided too little light, yet she ran through the woods, navigating them as though full sun shone upon her path.

Growling...

She heard growling.

* * * * *

Benjamin silently watched the slim line of her back as she disappeared, running away from him. With a weary sigh, he shifted from wolfman to full wolven form in the mere seconds it took for him to hit the floor. Stretching his long form out, his belly pressed the cool stone of the fireplace's hearth, and he rested his head on his paws.

"Well, I think she handled that rather well," Mal said into the silence.

Benjamin stared at him dolefully, the gleaming gold of his eyes speaking volumes.

Malachi chuckled and settled on the floor beside Benjamin, absently running a hand through the silky fur of Ben's mane. "Do not look so glum, Cross. She had a shock—just a shock. She will come around," he said softly, a slight smile canting his lips up. "Wait until she realizes what she is...or you tell her what I am," he said, his voice full of wry humor. "That will be the true test..."

Mal's voice trailed off and both vampire and wolf turned their heads, each cocking their heads and listening. The sounds were faint, very faint. Most likely nearly a mile away, a low growl, then the sounds of scrambling and struggle came drifting to them.

She was already letting the wolf inside her become part of her, speeding her movement, as she hurtled through the trees. They hadn't heard a human stumbling blind through the woods at night, just the occasional crash as a branch slapped at her, followed by total silence.

And then the growling.

A woman yelling now...screaming Ben's name.

Shadoe!

With a furious roar, Benjamin tore out of the house, Malachi moving in his wake like a silent wave of death.

The tableau before them was horrifying, Shadoe pinned to the ground by two men, a woman crawling all over her supine body, and Marcus standing against a tree, laughing as she screamed out in fury, blistering curses turning the air blue all around them.

"You're so much more...feisty than you used to be. I'm going to enjoy breaking you," Marcus announced.

A growl rent the air as Benjamin lunged, shifting from wolven form to wolfman in mid-leap, diving instinctively for Marcus. Out of the corner of his eye, he saw Malachi coming down on the two men holding Shadoe. Betas—weak insignificant betas—following the orders of their Alpha, and the bitch as she straddled Shadoe's body, pinching her soft, flat nipples and squeezing delicate flesh until she cried out in pain.

Malachi had already killed the first beta and as he tore the other one away from her, Shadoe threw the Inherent bitch away and lunged, taking her down and driving a fisted hand into the woman's surprised face.

Malachi stared up at the beta he had pinned against the trunk of a towering oak, opening his mouth in a wide smile and letting him see the deadly fangs. "Do you know what I am?" he purred.

Mal felt the fear that rolled through the small clearing as Benjamin Cross' rage spun out of control. One of an Inherent's most deadly skills was the paralyzing power of fear, creeping from them until it damned near froze the mind and body of their foes, leaving them totally helpless. The beta's eyes widened in uncontrolled terror and the hot, sour smell of urine filled the air.

"For pity's sake, Cross, how can I enjoy killing this bastard when you have him so shaking with fear, he does not even see me?" Malachi said drolly, tossing Benjamin an amused glance.

"My abject apologies," Benjamin snarled as he backhanded Marcus just when the weaker Alpha was lifting his head to howl, to call his wolves to him. With a deep sigh, he stopped radiating fear throughout, focusing instead on Marcus as he leaned forward and growled, "You touched my woman."

Rage enabled Marcus to throw the fear off and he rasped, "Mine. I saw her before you did—all but marked my claim in her tight little pussy. If you've fucked her, I'll kill you slow."

Benjamin laughed, the sound an odd, chuffing sort of gasp as he stared down at the lesser Inherent. "Too late—I've claimed her completely and she's *mine*. She all but killed you, you pathetic excuse for a wolf. You aren't worthy of her."

A furious howl fell from Marcus' lips and the struggle ensued as he tried to ram a hand up into Ben's throat, failing as the great wolfman powered him back down and lowered his head, snapping deadly fangs mere inches from Marcus' throat. "Consider yourself lucky I haven't already killed you…"

His voice trailed off as he sensed the odd surging of power in the clearing. Both heads swung to where Shadoe was standing over the pitifully sobbing female, her chest heaving as she glared down at the smallest of her attackers. The Inherent bitch still clung to human form, and her blonde hair was a bloody tangle around her face.

"Not my fault," she whimpered, her breath whistling through broken teeth. "He made me!"

Shadoe's skin rippled.

Cuffing his prey across the side of the head, Malachi warned, "If you move, I'll kill you slowly, instead of turning you over to the Council. You would much rather face them, believe me." Then he dropped the whimpering beta and turned his eyes to Shadoe, watching as she felt the change arc through her. Her back bowed.

"Stupid cunt—" Marcus snarled and he twisted, throwing Benjamin off in the brief second that Ben's eyes met Shadoe's over the distance. Benjamin turned to run after him, cursing himself for allowing his attention to wander, however briefly. But he stopped in his tracks as a soft sob filled the air.

The first change always hurt like a sonovabitch, worse than any other, because your mind was still clinging to the insistence it was human, and the fight was more painful for it.

He walked to her, slowly, carefully, releasing the wolfman form so that he stood in front of her in human skin, albeit very naked human skin, but he figured she was less likely to freak if he showed his dick, than if he stood there looking like…well, a wolfman.

"Shhh, sweet Shadoe," he rumbled against her ear as he drew her straining body against him. "Don't fight it. Please, just let it happen, and I'll help you through this."

"What is…happening?" she gasped, then she doubled over, knocking him back as her body started to spasm.

"Ahh..."

Malachi knelt beside her, lifting her up off the dirt, cradling her body against his, supporting her as Benjamin knelt in front of her, cupping her face in his hands, bending his brow down to rest on hers. Behind her, Malachi murmured, "It is just the change... Stop fighting it. This is what you are, nothing to fear."

"Benjamin..." the word left her in a strangled gasp as her heels scrambled against the ground. Her skin itched...it burned, aching, hot, tight. She screamed, throwing her head back, baring her throat, unaware of the heated, hungry look that started to fill Malachi's eyes.

"Oh, bloody hell, Benjamin," he rumbled, dragging air in.

Fur started to flow, and bones broke and reformed. Benjamin felt his throat lock as an agonizing scream filled the air. Smoothing his hand down the side of her face, he whispered, "Baby, it's almost over...almost over." And then it was and there was a beautiful wolf lying in his arms, her body shuddering. She had gone to full wolf, not stopping at the half-wolf, half-woman form, and the slimly built wolf in his arms weighed next to nothing. Her pelt was a golden brown, and her blue eyes gleamed as she lifted her head to stare at him.

"You're a shape-shifter," he said quietly, answering the question in her eyes. "That is what gave you the power, the strength to kill the man that was with Marcus all those years ago."

A soft whimper left her throat and Benjamin sighed, cuddling her close. "It's not permanent, not even a form you will want often, just when the urge to run overtakes you, when the wildness takes over. Just rest a while, and I'll help you back. I'm right here...right here."

Chapter Eight

Hours later, exhausted, Shadoe lay silent as Benjamin helped her between the sheets. Her eyes felt heavy, and her entire body ached. "Do I have to be like this?" she whispered. "Can't I just go back to what I was? I wanna be human."

"You were never human, Shadoe. Your mother wrapped spells around you to keep your true nature from showing, but what happened to you let everything inside you come out. It was all coming out in due time anyway, and now you've roused your true nature, love. You can't put it back inside a neat little package," he murmured, stroking her hair.

"But I don't know how to do this, I don't know where to go from here," she said, tucking her hand under her cheek as she rolled onto her side, staring out into the enveloping darkness. "How do I wake up every morning and just keep on writing, telling stories? It used to mean everything, mean my sanity. That was what Jillian did. Now…I just don't know. I don't know what I'm supposed to do."

"You don't have to *do* anything," he responded, pressing his lips to her temple. "Just be Shadoe."

Silence fell for a long while as she dealt with the burning inside her gut. "But Shadoe has to *do* something."

* * * * *

There was no doubt about it—she was one of them. Benjamin cuddled her sleeping body against his, the scent of her filling his head, the wonder of her filling his heart.

She was so damned perfect. The power that simmered under her skin left him stunned at times. She was full of power, full of magick.

And so uncertain of herself.

All of that made her vulnerable, and dangerous at the same time.

Tomorrow, it starts.

Closing his eyes, he was dimly aware of Malachi leaving as he followed her into dreams.

* * * * *

She woke in bed alone, her skin drawn tight, heat burning in her belly. The questions she had expected to find burning in her gut weren't there. But hunger was.

Ben's scent filled her head and her mouth watered. The image from last night of his long, golden body was burned on the inside of her eyelids and every time she closed her eyes, she saw him.

Curling her hands into fists, she pressed her nails into her palms, the sharp little pain doing nothing to clear the thick fog of need that clouded her mind. Slowly, she sat up and threw her legs over the side of the bed, breathing slowly.

She could smell him…and something else.

No, someone else.

Malachi.

That tall, pale giant with the streaming red banner of hair, and that sexy Scots burr.

They were downstairs, talking in low, hushed tones. The deep timbre of Benjamin's voice stroked over her, and she felt her nipples tighten and throb. Climbing from the bed in a dreamlike state, she padded down the stairs, following the aching in her gut. When she saw him, she crossed to him, and stopped his morning greeting with her mouth.

Malachi forgotten, she slid her hands inside Ben's open shirt, seeking hot, hard skin, the gleaming, smooth perfection of his chest vibrating under her hands as he moaned. Tearing his mouth from hers, he whispered, "Shadoe—"

Unable to think past the need in her gut, she whispered, "Hungry. Want you…" She slid her hands past the waistband of his jeans, restlessly stroking the skin she bared as she worked his jeans down.

"Shadoe—oh, damnation," Benjamin groaned, thought fleeing as her hot mouth closed over his aching cock. Bent over from the waist, her hair hanging in a curtain around her, she licked and sucked on his cock, making soft, mewling noises in her throat.

The hunger was on her, the driving sexual urges that could overtake an Inherent. It had hit her hard, and fast, and it was going to pull him under with her.

Gathering her hair in his fist, he stared with hungry, fascinated eyes as she moved her head up and down, the ruddied flesh of his cock disappearing between her lips with each downward stroke.

"Cross, you must think I am made of stone," a soft voice murmured. Benjamin lifted his gaze as he felt the jolt go through Shadoe, her mouth pulling away from his cock. Malachi's eyes were on her naked ass, bared by the shirt when she bent over. It slipped back into place as she straightened slowly, each move achingly sensual. When she turned and looked at Malachi, Benjamin saw something in her eyes, and jealousy tore through him. Wrapping his arms around her, one hand came up to cup a full round breast, the other hand roamed restlessly at her waist.

"Get out, Malachi," Benjamin groaned as Shadoe lowered her head and kissed his hand, her tongue darting out and caressing the skin. Benjamin pumped his cock against the firm curves of her ass, nestling it between the rounded cheeks, clenching his jaw, restraining the need to throw her down and mount her as he stared at Malachi.

Malachi laughed and said, "I hear that so very often. One of these days I will tire of hearing it."

Ben's hands were already busy on Shadoe's torso when Malachi turned and left. Her head fell back to rest on his chest, his hand slid down and cupped her cleft, grinding the heel lightly against her mound. Her heat flooded his hand, burning him, branding him, like he was dying to do to her.

Lowering his mouth and raking his teeth across Shadoe's exposed neck, he sank them in gently, beating back that urge to brand and mark. *Mine...mine... She is mine.* He knew it. He wanted her to know, he wanted the world to know. He wanted his mark on her for all the world to see.

Such a hard demon to fight, this crazed kind of lust. And now Shadoe's demon had come to the fore and he was powerless under the force of both.

He could smell her, the musk of her desire that was creaming in her pussy, the blood that was pounding hot and heavy in her veins. And he could hear her—the quick, hard beating of her heart, soft, excited breaths—each sound fueling his own desire.

Gripping her shirt in his hands, he tore it away. Grabbing her now naked hips, he bent her over the table. He stared hungrily at the exposed, wet folds of her cleft for a long second, licking his lips. Dragging his finger through the hot syrup, he lifted it to his lips, groaning in pleasure as the tangy taste exploded on his tongue.

Taking his cock in one hand, he aimed for the wet, exposed heart of her.

"Hold onto the table," he growled, kicking her legs apart after she had obeyed, licking his lips as a glistening pearl of cream trickled down from her pink, plump folds.

*Too fast...too fast...*he told himself, trying to focus on something besides burying his aching sex inside her and riding her until they both collapsed. But flowing from her was a wave of need and hunger, so deep, it nearly surpassed his.

"Damn it, Ben, please... I have to feel you inside me," she whimpered, wiggling her hips and pushing back against him.

"Not yet," he rasped, shaking his head, clearing the fog of lust so he could think. Everything was magnified. He could feel the ends of his hair whisper against his neck at the movement, everything multiplied and unbelievably clear as his hunger grew.

Closing his hand around his cock, he dropped to his knees behind her, catching that pearl with his tongue and savoring it. "Sweet, sweet Shadoe," he purred, pumping his cock slowly, teasing himself with the mental image of her pussy sliding up and down his cock in the same rhythm, up and down, over and over until he flooded her as she came around him with a scream.

Pressing his mouth against her, he spread her folds with a long, slow stroke of his tongue, and then he penetrated her, so that his tongue was sneaking into the heart of her, fucking in and out of her spasming core, as he cupped one cheek of her butt in his hand and spread her open to him.

In and out, slow, torturing strokes of his tongue until she was writhing against him, pushing back hungrily on him and whimpering, begging, pleading with him to fuck her.

Rising, he kissed a slow path up her spine, smoothing his hands over her hips, nestling his cock between the cheeks of her ass and pumping slowly, tears of pre-come seeping out to lubricate as he kept up the teasing torture.

"Damn it, fuck me," she demanded, pushing back hungrily. Her voice was low and rough with lust, and her skin was searing hot, hot enough to burn. The scent of her hunger was thick on the air, closing a tight fist around Benjamin's throat as he breathed it in.

He shifted his angle and breeched her pussy, sliding in just the first snug inch. "My pleasure," he murmured, bracing one hand on the base of her spine as he started to probe, pushing ever deeper inside her, slowly; the tight, silky inches of her closing over him like glory. Her wet heat spasmed around his cock and he growled, his lids dropping low over his eyes.

Hunkering over her bent form, he started to shaft her slowly, watching as his cock slid from her sheath, the dark flesh glistening from her cream. "You feel amazing, baby, you know that?" he muttered, surging back inside her. Her whimpered moan made his heart skip a few beats before it started to pound manically in his chest. *Mine...mine...mine...*

A soft keening cry tore from her lips as he started to drive harder and harder inside her, his pace keeping time with the raging beats of his heart. Reaching around, he pinched her clit, stroking it with firm, quick circles as she started to sob and plead mindlessly beneath him. "Mine," he growled, tweaking the hard, budded flesh of her clit.

She screamed as the climax hit her, the sleek muscles in her pussy clenching around his cock, milking him. Heat flared at the base of his spine and he gritted his teeth, holding the orgasm back, riding her harder and harder. He left off playing with her clit and started to stroke the puckered rosette with his cream-drenched fingers, slipping the tip of his finger inside her and feeling her jump. She clamped down harder around him, the rocking motions of her body freezing, her entire body going still.

Benjamin smiled, a hot, hungry smile as her head lowered, her spine curved down to the table and she started to whimper. Pushing deeper, he shuddered as the tight, virgin little hole locked down around him, trying to resist the slow, thorough possession of her ass. "You'll close over my cock so tight," he murmured. "I can make you feel so good."

Shadoe gasped, the air locked in her lungs, a scream building in her throat as he started to plunge his finger into her bottom with the same rhythm he pounded his cock into her aching core. Heat suffused her, tingling chills racing up and down her spine. She sobbed and pushed back against him, a tiny scream falling from her lips when that small movement took his teasing finger even deeper inside.

"You like that," he whispered, his deep, sexy voice an added caress against her. "You'll like it even more when I start to fuck you here, in your hot little ass. It's gonna drive you mad and you're gonna scream and beg for me. I'll slide my cock inside you, so slowly, we'll both damn near die from the pleasure before I'm buried inside you."

Hell, could she come just from him *telling* her about it?

Then she felt a second finger sliding in, stretching her. "Oh, hell," she sobbed, freezing, scared to move. She felt stretched too tightly, achingly full. Unconsciously, she pulled away as the hot, tingly chills coalesced into a bright burning nova, robbing her of the ability to think, to breathe. He surged deep inside, growling when she whimpered and tried to pull away.

"Mine," he rumbled, that deep, sexy voice stroking over her like a tangible caress. "You'll take it. Don't pull away from me. Feel it."

"Benjamin—" Her breath caught in her throat as he surged back inside. This time, he changed position so that the plum-shaped head of his cock was stroking over her G-spot.

"Come for me," he purred, working his fingers deeper and harder into her ass.

She fought it, clenching the muscles in her pelvis and trying to pull away, away from the deep pleasure-pain that shot through her with his every stroke.

"Come!" he barked, pulling out all the way to the head and driving back inside her with bruising force.

She screamed. She came. She writhed around his impaling cock, deep, harsh groans coming from her throat. A dam inside her broke and cream flowed from her in a river, bathing his cock, flowing out to coat his balls and trickle down her thighs. He removed his fingers from her ass and dug them into her hips, pulling her tightly against him. Shadoe felt a heated splash inside her, just at her G-spot, followed by the pulsating throb of his cock as he rode his climax to the end. "Perfect," he murmured, holding still within her, arching his spine, his head falling back.

A vibrant curse slid from his lips, followed by a long, shuddering groan and then his body came down, covering hers just briefly before he pulled her to the floor, cuddling her spine up against the front of his body, still locked inside her.

A shudder coursed through her as his cock pulsed again, teasing nerve endings that should be half dead by now. She whimpered, pushing her butt back against him. "Not enough," she whispered raggedly. "I need more…can't think…"

Benjamin pushed up onto his elbow, spilling her onto her belly. Taking her thigh, he opened her and lifted her leg up over his, keeping it there with a firm, demanding grip as he started to rock against her, tiny, teasing movements. She tried to push back against him and take more and he growled in warning. Falling still, hardly able to move in the position he held her body, Shadoe arched her hips just a little, clenching her muscles around him each time he stroked inside her, trying to hold him in.

An approving rumble left him with each little clutch of her pussy, until he was all but growling constantly. The sound fired her even more and she slid one hand up her torso, cupping her breast, pinching the hard, peaked nipple. "Benjamin, oh… *there*," she sobbed as he moved higher against her, now stroking over the buried nerve bed with each caressing stroke. "Harder, *harder*!"

"Mmmm, slow down, Shadoe," he purred. "There's no rush."

"The hell there isn't," she panted. "You're killing me."

He laughed and the sound vibrated down his body, his cock jerking within the snug embrace of her cleft. "I can't think of any better way to go than this, buried inside your sweet, wet pussy, feeling those little muscles stroking me, listening to you call my name when you come," he whispered, releasing her leg and hooking his hand over her mound, grinding his palm against her clit, pushing her hard back against him.

"Sweet," he praised, staring down at her body, a soft pink flush spreading up from her breasts, tinting her neck, coloring her cheeks. Her face lay cushioned on her palm, and she lifted her head slightly, staring at him over her shoulder, one rounded pink breast caught in the curve of her folded arm, the deep berry-colored nipple peeking out at him. "I can smell you, how hot, how hungry you are. It drives me insane."

His words stroked over her like a hand, drawing her tighter and tighter. "Ummm..." she whispered, her eyes glassy and bright with desire. "More...please."

With a feral grin, he started to pull out, then he surged hard back inside. The wet, sucking sounds from her pussy had him swearing, pulling out, driving back in, harder and harder until the slap of his flesh against hers filled the air, the scents of their combined hunger perfuming the heated room. Sweat gleamed on his body, the hard, convulsing muscles of his belly as he worked his cock into her sheath, gleaming on the rounded, bunched muscles at his shoulders, his arms, his back, all damp with sweat.

A harsh scream filled the air as she tightened around him again, a deep, spasming climax locking her pussy around his cock. He could barely work it back inside her as she rode the climax, her sheath tighter than a fist, wet, her tissues swollen from his hard thrusts.

"Mine," he gasped as he started to come, flooding her already wet depths with a hot stream of his seed before he collapsed against her, resting his brow on her shoulder. Little, minute shudders still racked her body, a soft whimper falling from her lips. "Perfect..."

It was past noon before the burning, driving hunger inside her core was briefly satisfied. Ben held her against him in the shower, his muscles feeling like putty, a dazed, sated feeling pumping through his veins with every beat of his heart.

She was nearly limp with exhaustion. As he worked scented suds through her hair, he murmured, "Don't sleep yet. You have to eat. Your body needs to refuel after last night...and this morning."

Lifting her head, she stared at him with a cloudy look in her pretty blue eyes. "What's going on? Why do I feel like I have to have you inside me every second of the day? You even speak and I want you again...or more. I can't stop wanting you," she mumbled, shaking her head.

A brief smile canted his lips up. "The wolf inside. She is hungry to mate, to be mated," he said. "She's been locked away from you all your life, unable to let her wishes be known. She's making up for lost time."

"She...?"

"The part inside you that made you change last night. Your subconscious, if you will. It makes you hungry, makes you want... It is what guided you through the change last night when you were attacked. It's the animal within you." He watched her face as he spoke, looking for some sign of revulsion or disgust. He saw only a weary resignation.

"Will it always be like this?" she asked plaintively.

He chuckled and cuddled her against him. "No. The wolf is merely stamping her mark on you. Soon, you'll be able to beat her back into submission, letting her out only when needed. But for now, I wouldn't fight it."

Good thing, Shadoe thought later as she stared at the heaping plate of food Benjamin had slid under her nose. She wouldn't have been able to fight this anyway, not now. Not yet. She was weak, tired, exhaustion permeating every inch of her being.

And still...as she watched him return to the stove to toss fluffy eggs, golden brown biscuits and crispy bacon onto his own plate, she wanted him. Still. His tight, perfect butt in his snug jeans caught her eye, and she had to clench her nails into her palms to keep from reaching out and grabbing him.

Welcome, little sister...

Shadoe jerked, her fork falling unnoticed to the floor.

A voice.

She heard a voice.

A soft, amused noise flooded her system, filling her, echoing around her. Like *laughter*...but not from a human throat.

Long have you been gone to me, the voice whispered. *For a time, I knew it had to be so, but then… I missed you, and tried to call to you, but the barrier between you and me was thick. I couldn't breach it. A powerful woman, she must have been…*

Who? Shadoe wondered, her eyes wheeling around the room, looking for the one who spoke to her.

"Your mother," Benjamin answered. Turning, he met her eyes and moved across the room, setting his plate on the table before coming to kneel beside her, taking one of her stiff, cold hands in his. Then he glanced around the room, as though searching for something. "Wolf…be nice. She's had a rough time lately."

That odd, chuffing sort of laughter again and then the voice came, but this time it was aloud, not just spoken within her. "Brother…am I ever not nice?" the creature asked in a purring sort of rumble.

Ben laughed. "Stop playing games, Wolf. Bad enough she has to deal with this animal you've unleashed running rampant within her. She doesn't need a cocky totem making things worse," he said.

"It is not an animal within her…it is my essence." The voice was haughtier now, and smug. Then she sensed a sort of softening in this presence, a fondness, and something almost like an invisible hug settled over her shoulders. "My pretty, precious sister," the being whispered lovingly. "Listen…learn…*feel*…"

Shadoe's breath locked within her throat as she was pulled out of her body, and she could feel herself being flung through time and space. Then a soft grayness took her and she could think of nothing else.

Floating infinitely inside that warm gray cocoon, Shadoe felt bathed in love, warmth, acceptance. Then she felt *solid* again and her eyes opened. But she wasn't in her home.

A forest, vast and ageless, surrounded her, and everything around her shimmered with life. The trees, the moss growing on the tumbled rocks—those very rocks seemed to gleam with life.

And lying in front of the rocks was a massive gray wolf, his eyes deep satiny pools of silver, unlike any wolf she had ever seen or imagined.

"Welcome, sister, to the dreamscape."

Although the wolf's mouth didn't move, the words came from him.

At her back, she felt a warm, familiar presence and then Ben's hands came up, gripping her shoulders, holding her firmly against him, a solid, silent pillar of support.

"Duh…dream…dreamscape?" she stuttered.

"My home within."

"Within what?" she asked, jumping when her voice echoed, vibrating around her, filling her.

"Within you, within Benjamin…within every creature that I have blessed with my touch and who listens to my call."

Her eyes were confused. "Blessed… You mean, people who can change, like Ben? Like me? Like…"

The Wolf studied her, his eyes gentle, understanding. "Marcus is a being who has my touch, through the blood of his parents. He can shift from wolf to man, like you. But he is no longer mine. He cannot feel my touch, or know the greater powers I can bless my brethren with. Although, I do torment him from time to time and make him hear my voice. He strayed, long ago. He is corrupt. Foul…and he has to die. Will you do it?"

Her mouth went dry. "Me?"

Rising, the great pony-sized wolf padded over to her. "Yes… You. You have the power, the skill…even the knowledge of how evil he is and why he must die. He seeks to breed and mate, taking as many women as he can…seeking the mindless, the easily controlled. His sickness may well bear weight on his young — that cannot be allowed. Would you see him do to others what he has tried to do to you?"

"I can't just kill somebody. That's murder," she whispered.

"Not in battle, it is not," the Wolf murmured, nuzzling her thigh with his head.

Against her ear, Benjamin whispered, "That is justice. That is what the Hunters do."

"I am not a Hunter," she whispered, hardly able to think of this near-mythical group of men and women who battled in the night.

Benjamin cuddled her back against him and asked quietly, "Aren't you?"

The words from last night came to her, unbidden. *But Shadoe has to* do *something.*

A sense of purpose, of necessity had started to bud inside her heart in those confusing, life-altering moments of the past night, as Benjamin guided her from wolf form to human skin.

Shadoe has to do *something.*

Lifting her eyes, she met the fathomless gaze of the Wolf. In that gaze, she saw an understanding, an acceptance that she had never felt before.

She saw *home*.

Chapter Nine

Malachi stopped dead in his tracks.

Bloody hell.

Both Benjamin and Shadoe were frozen in the kitchen, eyes staring, as though gazing at each other in wonder.

But the odd tingle in the air told him otherwise, even before he had thoroughly taken in their motionless stance. Sighing, he settled on the counter, drawing one knee up to his chest and resting it there. Long, long moments passed and still the two Inherents remained motionless, their eyes blank and unseeing.

"You know, you blasted bloody mongrel," Malachi said mockingly. "This could be so very dangerous for them, pulling them under like this, keeping them so unaware."

He sensed amusement filling the air around him. Then, shockingly, spoken words... "As if I would leave what is mine in danger."

Malachi grinned. A rare honor, having the protective spirit talk to one who wasn't his.

Nearly an hour later, a great sigh seemed to fill the room and the Inherents stirred, eyes blinking, bodies stretching, shifting around. Cocking a brow at them, Malachi said, "Have a nice chat?"

Benjamin couldn't actually claim surprise at Malachi's apparent knowledge of the Wolf. The blasted ancient one had been around for centuries untold, and it seemed there was very little about the world of the Hunters he didn't know. Later, as Shadoe slept, her body still trying to adapt to the changes thrust upon it, he passed by the door leading to the basement.

Malachi slept down there...or rested. Fortunately, the family room was down there, and the old couch she had would hold him better than the twin bed in the only other furnished bedroom.

That would be another shock to hand her, he thought in disgust. It wouldn't bode well for her to see one of her compatriots fighting alongside her suddenly grow fangs as he attacked an enemy.

Wouldn't sit too well with her.

Although she had taken every surprise in stride. Ben was wondering if maybe she hadn't realized, somewhere inside her, that she had never been normal, never been just like everybody else around her. The books he had been sending her over the years revealed more of the unspoken world and hopefully, she had absorbed some of the matter-of-fact images and language in which the books were written.

Her life had so suddenly changed. Too many times such changes were too traumatic for the average human to bear. How many had not survived the insanity of such changes?

Hundreds of thousands, over the centuries. Suicide was high among their kind, the Hunters, the vampires. For the witches and the Inherents, it was less so, because they had been born into their powers, and most were raised to know they would walk a different path, even if they didn't become a Hunter. The Hunters were the elite, the few, policing the world to watch for the monsters that became even more insane when the changes of werewolf or vampire came down upon them. The rest of the unspoken world lived as normally as most humans, working, marrying, having families. But the witches, Inherents, and shape-shifters who were born, not made, often kept to themselves, to their packs. Always with the knowledge that they were something different.

But for a vampire or the created werewolf, those whom had the change forced upon, life could become a dark and lonely place. Sanity was pushed to the limit and it often broke, casting the person in a maelstrom of violence, too often into a realm where the person was locked into themselves, too depressed to continue their life, as it was.

Thus, suicide.

Or too often, homicide, as the ferals started to prey upon mortal kind to briefly sate their pain.

That Shadoe was taking this in stride so easily mystified him.

Why, brother?

Benjamin started as the Wolf woke and sensed his discomfort, his confusion. *You have been preparing her for this, the best you can, since you first learned of her whereabouts. Part of her had already accepted that she was different, that something unknown had happened when she killed the cruel bastard who attacked her. You've just been guiding her down the path of knowledge.*

She will be fine, the Wolf assured him, whispering quietly, comfortingly into his mind.

"How can a handful of books give her that confidence?" Ben asked.

Not just the books...the acceptance. You already accepted her and the part of her that is mine acknowledged that. Your being here when she was released further confirmed that. She isn't alone in this world. You've made sure of it.

Benjamin dropped onto the couch, staring sightlessly up at the ceiling. Golden-brown eyes closed as he pressed his hands to his face, sighing raggedly.

"It's not that easy. It can't be."

The Wolf chuffed with amusement. *Of course it can. The harder parts are yet to come. The question is...who will it be harder for? Her or you?*

Before Benjamin could puzzle that one, the Wolf was gone, leaving Benjamin in the silence.

* * * * *

"First, you will learn to fight..." Benjamin had told her when she woke with the knowledge that she would kill Marcus.

"You must prey upon something that is lesser than Marcus, while we teach you how to use this newfound strength of yours. A soldier doesn't go into battle on his first day in the Army," he had insisted. "Later, we will hunt down Marcus...when you are ready."

So they walked the streets of St. Louis. Hours from home, but both Ben and Malachi had insisted. She'd find nothing in her hometown that would help her.

"All the lesser monsters, human or otherwise, will flee when a badder bastard comes to town," Malachi informed her. "There is nothing worth Hunting here. Marcus has seen to that. Those who aren't his are long gone or long dead."

"Hunting...you mean, killing," she said faintly as she walked between Benjamin and Malachi.

"Some people are worth killing," Mal said enigmatically. His long, powerful arm lifted and gestured to the alley across the way. "Like there..."

She heard it, an odd scrabbling sound that made no sense to her ears. But the soft strangled cry did.

She didn't even remember running but now she stumbled to a halt, frozen at the sight before her. A woman lay cowering on the ground, kicking at the hands that sought to restrain her. A bloody, dirty cloth had been shoved into her mouth, muffling her cries. That was what the soft, strangled noise had been, her fighting to scream around her gag.

Shadoe saw red.

Benjamin had to force himself to hold back as Shadoe lunged, her small, compact form hurtling through the air as she took down the man who wasn't fighting to hold the woman still. He had been too busy unfastening his jeans and smirking at the woman's distress and fear.

Human monsters. Not a spark of magick in them, not a touch of wolven power.

Just human monsters who preyed on the weak. "I told you not to go to the cops, bitch," the man was saying. "I warned...oomph—" His words were broken off as Shadoe took him, snarling viciously, her pretty face tight with anger, her eyes flashing with it.

Skin rippled and this time the change was quicker, from human to wolfwoman, and she snapped out with her teeth as the man started to scream in fear.

"How does it feel?" she asked haltingly, forcing the words through her alien mouth.

Malachi moved in, blocking the other woman's eyes, catching her gaze and murmuring, "Sleep..." When her body went limp, he looked at the man holding her arms and said coolly, "Let her go."

"What the fu..." The man was paying no attention to Malachi, instead staring at the furred, lithe form crouched atop his friend's prone body.

"Do not worry about her," Malachi whispered evilly. "Worry about *me*."

"You waste too much time talking," Ben said absently, flicking his wrist as he gathered the wind elements in the air, directing them to the bastard who held the woman's feet, eagerly shoving her thighs apart, almost as if he was unaware of the danger around them.

He was jerked up and away, pinned to the wall by magick. Benjamin smiled at him, a nasty smile that made the blood run cold.

Malachi said, "Are you going to fuss at me if I play with my food?"

"Mind your manners, Mal," Benjamin said drolly as he released the wind elements. Obeying him, the elements dropped the struggling man to his feet, some four feet below, and he landed with a crash, only to swarm back up, drawing a wicked six-inch switchblade from his pocket.

"Now, you really want to put that away before you piss me off," Benjamin murmured, nimbly moving out of reach as the man slashed out with the blade. "I'll be supremely pissed if you cut me."

"As will I," Mal added as he snapped the neck of the man right after the pathetic creature tried to swing at him. "I imagine all that lovely blood will be wasted."

Benjamin flicked a glance at Shadoe, who was pummeling the man, back in her gleaming, naked hide, unaware of anything around them. "She doesn't know about you just yet—care to keep the appetizer and meal comments down?"

Then he kicked out, driving his heel into the man's unprotected belly, the blade narrowly missing Benjamin's chest.

The man hit the wall, struck his head, and fell to the ground, unconscious. Malachi grinned and said, "We really need to let her know, and soon. I could have used the snack."

Then he nudged the man with the broken neck and a frown crossed his face. "Then again, maybe not. He reeks."

Shadoe's arm lifted but before she could hit the now unconscious man, it was caught and held firmly. "I think he gets the point, sweet," Ben drawled, cocking a brow at her.

He was an unconscious bloody mess, air whistling in and out of a surely broken nose. His chest rose and fell fitfully.

"Oh, sweet heaven, what have I done?"

"Justice."

Shadoe looked up as Malachi slid out of the shadows, the woman cuddled in his arms, unbelievably sleeping. "They would have raped her, passed her around like a rag doll, and killed her," Malachi said, rubbing his cheek against the woman's tangled black hair. "All because she went to the police about this bastard selling drugs to children."

"You've done justice," he reiterated, a dark look entering his eyes as he stared at the bloody waste of the man beneath Shadoe.

She rose slowly. "How do you know what he has done?" Her eyes moved to the listless, woman in his arms, her head slumped forward in the position of deep sleep, her skin pale, bruises ringing her wrists now, bloody scrapes marring the ivory flesh of her face and legs.

"From her. She holds the knowledge in her mind, and when I touched her mind to make her sleep, I saw the answers," Malachi said obliquely.

"How can you touch her mind?"

He smiled gently. "I do not think you need any more shocks dealt you right now, pet," he murmured. Studying the woman with unreadable eyes, he said, "I will take my leave now...she needs medical care. There is a cousin of hers not far from here."

Shadoe hadn't so much as blinked before he was gone. Her eyes met Benjamin's, large, far too dark in her face, full of fear and confusion. "I almost killed him," she whispered raggedly. Her eyes moved to the unconscious man, and she would swear she could hear his heart beating, the breath moving raggedly in and out of his chest, whistling through his busted nose and swollen mouth.

His eyes were still closed, discolored and swelling, turning that deep blue-purple of a new bruise. Blood that had flowed from his nose in a gush was drying on his skin in a nasty maroon red smear, streaked with mucus. What bothered her the most was that it *pleased* her to see him like that. Hot satisfaction filled her and she couldn't stop it, even though she knew it was wrong to have so enjoyed hurting a man.

But this man was worse than an animal, less than human. She could sense evil in him, a desire to hurt, to prey upon the weak. She rubbed her arms, and saw with surprise that she was naked, the shreds of a shirt clinging to her arms, the rest of her clothes lying in tatters around her. From changing. The wolf form was so much larger, so much more powerful, it had torn apart the clothes she was wearing when she changed.

But before she could even begin to puzzle out what to do about it, Benjamin shrugged a backpack off his shoulder and tugged out a pair of jeans and a T-shirt, his eyes hot on her body as he approached, holding them out to her. After she took them, he lifted one finger and traced it around a budded pink nipple in a slow circle.

Then his hand dropped away and he clenched it into a fist, before turning away. "Get dressed before I start something we can't finish," he muttered. "This isn't the time or place."

Heat pooled in her belly at the sound of his gruff voice, her nipples tightening to the point of pain, her cleft starting to weep with want. Tugging the shirt over her head, she shuddered as the cotton abraded her bare breasts. As she zipped the jeans, a weak whimper left her lips, because the seam of the jeans was rubbing against her naked folds, and each movement teased her clit against the rough cloth.

Lifting smoky eyes, she stared at Benjamin as he walked through the tiny alley, collecting the shreds of her clothes and stowing them in the backpack before tossing it over his shoulder.

Their eyes met and she felt the look like a caress, stroking over her unfettered breasts, down her torso, onto her belly, down to the apex of her thighs where she ached and hungered for him. Ached to feel the hard, hot drive of his cock inside her, filling her, fucking her until they both screamed at the pleasure of it, and then doing it all over again, and again until they collapsed.

She licked her lips, her body quivering.

As one, they turned their gazes when the man on the ground started to shift, and move. He moaned, a choked, garbled sound and his lids started to lift, a slow struggle due to the pain he was in. Wrapping her arms around herself, she watched as Benjamin approached him, cocking his head and smiling a gentle, terrifying smile.

"How does it feel?" Benjamin purred, crouching down until he was on level with the man's eyes. The pain-filled, terrified eyes met Benjamin's and in his stupor, he didn't realize that Benjamin was the enemy.

"Dude…hurts…fucking bitch… Is she gone? How…"

Benjamin smiled and from her position, she could see it as his teeth started to lengthen, almost like a Hollywood-style vampire, a spine-tingling, frightening beauty that made him cower on the pavement even more. "What…what are you?"

Benjamin ignored him as he asked, "Does it hurt? Do you enjoy how it feels to be at the mercy of something that is so much stronger than you?"

"Help!" The shout was pitiful, choked, barely more than a strangled yelp. Turning his eyes back to Benjamin, he begged, "Don't…please don't."

Benjamin grinned, displaying that deadly, toothy grin and reaching up to stroke his chin with a hand that now displayed long, deadly hooked claws. "Don't? You plead with me? You beg? Like the woman begged, like she screamed for help and you laughed." His voice dropped to a low whisper and Benjamin murmured, "I cannot kill in cold blood and you are helpless against us now. But I won't allow you to ever harm another woman, another creature."

In a lightning quick movement, he reached out, seizing the man's face in his hands and squeezing, as his lids drooped. A harsh whisper that Shadoe couldn't comprehend escaped Ben's mouth and the battered man on the ground screamed, arching his back up as his feet scuttled on the ground for purchase.

Shadoe had no more than blinked when Benjamin moved away from the man and now stood at her side, a hard, grim set to his mouth. "He has an evil mind. Very evil," he murmured. "His punishment shall be very, very long."

"His punishment?" she echoed, confused.

Benjamin smiled. "He's caught in a loop. For every wrong he has done, it will come back to him. Only in his mind, but it will seem so very real. And it will continue until he breaks it himself, by acknowledging his evil and stopping it, regretting it, seeking atonement. Only true repentance can free him, as true repentance should free anyone. But that will never happen. Not for him."

"So he will just live like that?" Shadoe asked, staring as the man tried to curl into his body, pleading and whimpering like a child one moment, then bellowing with rage as he threatened to eat the heart of some unknown assailant.

"Hmm. Until he has had enough most likely, and ends it."

Shadoe suspected ending it meant ending his life.

Yes, it was a fitting punishment for the man whose evil still clung to her skin, making her feel dirty.

"Is this what I will do? How I will live?"

Benjamin studied her with quiet eyes and simply responded, "You tell me."

She let him drive her home, or at least to the outskirts of town. But then she jumped out of the van, ignoring his voice and she left, walking away as fast as her feet could carry her. The confusion that filled her brain made an answer impossible. Benjamin didn't follow her, and she no longer worried about walking the streets alone at night. She had become something more dangerous than any scumbag trolling the streets.

Circling through the streets, wandering aimlessly as she tried to filter all the new information, all the new problems she now had facing her. It was nearly three hours later when she arrived at her doorstep, in the dead of night, midnight already passed, dawn not even a dream upon the horizon.

Opening the door, she froze as something assaulted her senses, heating her blood, stroking over her like a velvet hand. Her heart kicked into high gear and she whimpered as cream flooded her pussy before she even knew what was going on.

Breath locked in her throat, she closed the door behind her and took a step further into her house, quivering with each tiny movement. Sounds made themselves known to her. A low, husky male voice crooning, a woman's pleasure-filled moan, wet sucking sounds that had her vagina clenching in recognition.

Another slow, shaking step, then another and another until she stood in the arch that opened into her living room. On the floor, Malachi was sprawled next to a petite, dark-eyed brunette, his tongue circling around her nipple, his hand between her thighs.

As Shadoe watched, his fingers slid out, wet and shining, and then he pushed those two fingers back inside. Closing his lips around her nipple, he suckled hungrily, and the woman arched up against him, her fingers sliding through his hair, her hips lifting to meet his hand.

"Come, Melissa…come for me. Come…"

Shadoe jolted when Malachi rolled his eyes to stare at the woman, his gaze hot and hungry. As she watched, the woman started to come and Malachi lifted his head, moving his lips up to her neck. His head arched back, and Shadoe froze, her heart stuttering to a stop. There were *fangs* in his mouth, not the jagged, ripping teeth she had seen in Ben's mouth, but two long incisors, and she watched numbly as he pierced the woman's flesh with those teeth, before fastening his lips around the freely flowing blood source.

She lunged, and the movement had Malachi lifting his head, a startled "*Fuck*" escaping him before he rolled to his back to catch Shadoe and move her away from the still screaming woman.

Her screams of ecstasy reduced to sobs as her body trembled and arched up, as though seeking a cock to fill her. Malachi tossed her a short look and whispered, "Sleep," before he lifted his eyes to the woman he had on top of him, wrapping his arms around her and staring irately into her eyes.

"Do you mind? I haven't had a good feed in weeks," he snapped, a scowl twisting that perfect mouth, now swollen and red. At the corner, she saw a drop of blood and that only enraged her further.

"Fucking monster," she snarled in a hiss, jerking angrily in his arms, trying to dislodge him.

"I am not," Malachi snapped indignantly. "I'm a bloody vampire... There's a difference."

Shadoe shuddered as his cock pulsed at the exposed vee of her thighs. The jeans covering her might as well have not been there as he transferred her wrists to one hand so that he held her in a secure grip, leaving one hand free to cup her ass and hold her still as he pumped against her.

"Malachi," a low, rough growl trickled into the room and Shadoe froze. The hand holding her wrists released them and she sat up slowly, staring down at Malachi's beautiful, hard face, his midnight blue eyes glowing with a hunger that had her belly clenching.

"Your woman called me a bloody monster and flew at me while I was having my first good meal in weeks," Malachi said, grinning at Benjamin, his eyes hot and wicked.

His hands lay on her thighs, not restraining her, just resting there as though testing her. When she still sat motionless, his hands moved higher, higher, until his thumbs met in the middle over the throbbing bud of her clit. Circling, scraping, pressing, each slow stroke drawing her tighter and tighter, until she was rocking hungrily against those strokes.

"You're touching my woman, Malachi," Benjamin growled.

"Your woman wants to be touched," Mal murmured, watching her face with rapt eyes. Her head lifted and she tracked the ragged sound of Benjamin breathing, held in place by the fire in his eyes.

Her body arched and she sobbed as the hunger that she had thought was sated returned full force.

"The wolf's hunger is on her," Malachi whispered. "Fuck me, but she's lovely wi' it."

Benjamin's eyes moved over her face and his cock started to swell, his own lust roused by hers, mixed with a mad desire to fuck and possess her like she had never been possessed before.

He crossed to her, stalking them, each move slow and deliberate as he knelt behind her, one knee on each side of Malachi's legs. Cupping her hips, he jerked her back against him, the surprised, aroused little gasp from her drawing his gut tight. He pumped his cock against the soft curve of her ass as he lowered his head to her neck, raking the delicate skin with his teeth.

Malachi moved his fingers over her clit, over and over, circling, pressing, and she started to rock her hips, back and forth, between the magick of Malachi's wicked fingers and the pulsating pressure of Ben's cock against her ass. Shadoe's head fell back as Ben's hands slid up her sides, cupping her breasts, plumping them together, tweaking the nipples, milking them. Malachi watched with hooded eyes, the dark blue of his gaze swirling, shifting, gleaming with a deep light under the fringe of his lashes.

Shadoe sobbed as Malachi's fingers worked her closer and closer to the precipice, arching under Benjamin's hands, his teeth sinking into the skin of her shoulder, marking her.

Benjamin and Malachi both stilled as a soft, sighing breath came to them, but Shadoe was unaware, riding the hand between her thighs, working her clit up against it, wishing her clothes were *gone* and she was pressed between the two men.

Their eyes moved to the sleeping woman only feet away from them.

"You have something you need to attend to, Malachi," Benjamin growled. Shadoe cried out as his arms closed around her and he rolled them clear of Malachi, ending with her sprawled on her belly and Benjamin half-draped over her.

Malachi said slyly, "I think your woman would like us both to attend to her." His eyes met Shadoe's as she turned her face to his voice, her body clamoring once more for the stroke of his fingers against her clit.

Ben's face split with a hot, slow smile as he gripped the waistband of her jeans. "Then you had better hurry," he responded softly as he tore her jeans away.

Malachi's eyes widened and his face went stark with hunger as he stared at Shadoe's prone form.

And then the vampire was gone so fast neither Benjamin nor Shadoe could track his movement. Alone in the room, Benjamin finished tearing away the shreds of her jeans, reaching for her shirt next, ripping it with one hard jerk, before he leaned over her body and whispered, "You let him touch you. You wanted it..." Covering her body with his, he pinned her hands down and purred, "I hope you are ready to deal with the consequences."

He plunged his finger deep into her pussy and she gasped, rocking against him only to have him pull away. Her eyes opened with terrified arousal as he started to probe between the cheeks of her buttocks, seeking out the rosette there and pressing insistently against her until it opened and he sank his lubricated finger in. Pushing past the tight ring of muscle, and working in and out, he pumped and rotated his wrist as he stretched her.

She shrieked and tried to pull away, the hot, burning desire mixing with fear as her skin grew tighter and hotter and her hunger spun out of control. "Naughty girl," Benjamin whispered, lifting his hand and bringing it down with stinging force on her naked ass. "You wanted it—you're gonna get it. We have to get this tight little ass of yours opened for me."

She sobbed at the painful pleasure of it as he sank his finger deep inside, the flesh clutching at his penetration, spasming around it, trying to hold him out, or keep him inside.

It was bad...it was naughty...it was so unbelievably good, Shadoe couldn't think past it.

Electricity seemed to fill the air around them, smothering them, and they both lifted their heads as Malachi materialized in front of them, still naked, his cock hard and thick against his belly as he dropped to his knees at her side.

Wrapping one arm around her waist, Ben lifted her up, revealing her naked body. With a steady, driving rhythm, he continued to work his fingers in her ass, until she started to push her hips back, seeking more. Malachi's long-fingered, graceful hands—a warrior's hands, a poet's hands—came up, cupping her face as he lowered his mouth to hers, stealing her breath as he drove his tongue inside with no preliminaries, setting up a rhythm that matched Ben's thrusts into her rear. One hand, cool and hard, left her face and cupped her, and he pushed his finger inside her pussy as he circled his thumb over her clit.

Shadoe screamed, coming in a hard, body-racking shudder, writhing between them as she pumped herself up and down, riding the orgasm through to the end.

Benjamin's hands left her and his presence withdrew. Not seeing the nod that passed between them, she mewled, aching for the loss of his heat, even as Malachi fell to his back, taking her with him as he kissed her deeply, stealing more of her taste, swallowing her down.

"Benjamin," she whispered, pulling her mouth away and trying to lift her head.

"Shhh," Malachi purred. He started to move beneath her, working his rigid, pulsating cock back and forth between her slick folds, caressing her clit. The rustling of clothes being removed came to her, although she could hardly make sense of it. The aching hunger inside her robbed her of thought, and all she wanted was to feel it again, the sensation of their bodies crowding her, stroking hers, bringing her to mind-shattering climax.

Benjamin's hands were on her waist again now, and she cried out with pleasure at the heat of his nude body. Something cool and wet spread over the tight pucker of her ass and then worked inside, in and out, until she was well lubricated. Her eyes met Malachi's and he whispered, "He's gonna sink his cock into tha' sweet, pretty ass of yours, nice an' slow, then I'll fuck me own cock into yer soft little pussy. Och, twill be good, better than good…"

His voice was thickened now by a heavy Scots accent and the rough sensuality of his words and his voice stroked over her, adding to the myriad sensual delights she was drowning in.

Something flooded the air, flooded her, a hot velvet stroke of sensation unlike any she had ever known, and her eyes locked on Mal's. An urge, heavy and insistent filled her, the urge to sink her pussy down on his cock and ride him until she could no longer move.

"Vampire!" Ben's harsh bark barely filtered through the haze of desire that surrounded her.

"We canna let her feel the pain, Cross," he rasped, his lids low, hooded, eyes locked on her face. "She's never taken two men at once. D'ya want to hear her cry out in pain?"

"This is my woman," Benjamin growled, and he jerked her ass back to meet his body as he spoke.

"Then give her what she wants and I'll keep her from hurting for it," Malachi snapped, his hand fisted in her hair, keeping her head up when she would have wilted against him. "Watch me, pet…watch me…"

His hand slid between their bodies and he started to tease her clit, circling over it with quick, darting touches, retreat and stroke, over and over until she was rocking her hips back and forth to meet each caress.

Benjamin growled and gripped her hips, holding her still as he started to probe her ass, butting the head of his cock against the tight little hole, the sensation of his heated flesh sliding, moving just barely against her driving her mad. She pushed eagerly back against him, and shuddered as he stilled the teasing motions and started to possess.

The hard, thick head pressed against the hole until it flowered open around him, and he worked the first inch inside.

Her lids closed as the delirious pleasure arced through her. But the moment her eyes left Malachi's, the pain returned and she whimpered, her body stiffening. "No, damn it," Benjamin growled, holding her hips still and steady as he pushed another inch inside. "You *will* take it. Hold her eyes, Mal."

"Watch me," the vampire purred, and she stared at him mesmerized, as his eyes started to glow, the dark blue midnight gaze turning to sapphire jewels in his hard, handsome face. Circling his thumb over her clit, he stroked her with fast, firm circles, using his body and the vampire's call to hold her in thrall as Benjamin pushed deeper inside her.

She shuddered, her body arching as she moved helplessly against their restraining hands. "You're tighter than a fist," Benjamin panted. "Hot, silky…*mine*. Remember that, as he fucks his way into your pussy… *You are mine…*"

Shadoe screamed as he sank home and the pain of it burned through her despite Malachi's gaze holding her prisoner. It bloomed into a dark, burning pleasure that robbed her breath as she writhed and bucked under his hands.

He pulled out and sank back in, slow and steady, three times before he stilled and said, "Fuck her, Malachi." Bending over her prone body, he whispered, "You wanted this…take it, take *me*."

Malachi grunted at the tight clasp of her pussy on his cock as he slowly forged through the tissues, feeling Benjamin's throbbing presence just beyond the delicate membrane between them. "Fuck me, you are tight," he gasped, his eyes slitted, his neck arched back as he sought to control the urges that flooded him.

She was wet, creamy, and every breath she took vibrated through her and caressed his cock, humming down his length, tightening his balls. Staring into her eyes, he purred, "Tha's the way, pet. Damnation, y' feel good. Hot, tight, snug little pussy. Take more…"

Arching his hips up, he worked his length deeper, listening to her mewling, her nails digging bloody little crescents into his shoulders. Once he was buried to the balls inside her, he stilled and then Benjamin moved. Then Malachi…then Ben…alternating thrusts that filled her full. The tight hot thrusts of Ben's cock, then the warming presence of Mal's, each a counterpoint to the other.

She screamed, cream flooding from her, her vagina going into spasms around Mal's cock, her ass clenching at Ben's swollen length as she came and they continued to fuck her. Fucking their cocks past the tight, convulsing tissues, Benjamin panted, swearing as sweat dripped off of him, and Malachi arched his powerful body, driving up into her pussy with bruising force.

She came again before she had even caught her breath from the first, and Benjamin swore, his hand lifting and coming down on her ass with stinging force as he panted, "Again, sweet heaven, damn it, Shadoe…tight, hot, sweet little fuck."

He drove into her, harder and harder, and Shadoe sobbed, her teeth sinking into her lip, cutting it. Malachi's hands caught her face and he crooned, "Hmm… dessert…" as he sucked the oozing cut on her lip. He rotated his hips against hers, pumping in and out, sliding his hand between them and finding her clit.

She shivered as he stroked it, pulling with them as each man started to work his cock harder and harder into her, each one nearing orgasm. As Benjamin sank his thick length inside her one last time, she screamed, light exploding in front of her, stealing her breath away like a fist plowing into her gut. The shudders racked her body and she screamed long and loud and then darkness blanketed her and took her down.

Malachi fucked harder and harder into her pussy even as she passed out, grunting as her still convulsing sheath stroked over his aching penis. The sensation raced down his spine and he exploded into her, bucking hard enough to nearly throw Ben and Shadoe from him.

Benjamin snarled as he held firm, riding his climax through to the end before he sank down, rolling to his side, taking Shadoe with him. Mal rolled with them, keeping his cock snug inside her, and both men cuddled her body between them.

An hour later, she woke. A hot washcloth was working back and forth inside her pussy and her face flamed as she saw Malachi toss it aside before catching her hips in his hands and lowering his mouth to her cleft. She flinched at the sight of elongated fangs and he purred, "Not to worry, pet... I won't bite...unless you ask."

His tongue pierced her folds, his nose nuzzling her clit. She heard the shower but couldn't think and recall what it was. Then Benjamin was in the doorway and he asked, "Getting started without me?"

Malachi rumbled, "Having a treat, go fuck yourself," before catching her clit between his teeth and sucking. Benjamin laughed as he flung his body down on the floor next to Shadoe, cupping her chin and lifting her mouth to his. "No...I'm gonna fuck her. Be nice and I might share."

Shadoe's mouth fell open and she wanted to snap at Ben but Malachi's tongue chose that moment to dance over her clit in a particularly clever fashion and she whimpered, deciding she'd rather like being shared again.

Strong arms came around her waist and she shrieked as Malachi stood, his arms under her ass, holding her full weight on level with his mouth as he fucked his tongue inside her sheath, shifting her thighs so that she had one knee on each of his shoulders.

Benjamin rose slowly, closing his fist around his cock, pumping as he watched the vampire eat at her cream-drenched pussy until she came with a flood, the sharp scent of her climax heavy in the air.

Taking her around the waist, Benjamin lifted her down, turning her, before he lifted her this time, and drove his cock inside her still convulsing pussy. "Did you like how it felt when he ate you?" he whispered against her lips as he lifted her up and down on his impaling cock.

She whimpered, her face flaming.

"Did you?"

"Yes," she sobbed.

Malachi was at her back now, and she shuddered when she felt his cool, slick fingers working over her, inside her, lubricating her anal passage inside and out.

"Let him feed from you as we fuck you, baby," Benjamin whispered.

"No," Malachi growled. He grasped the back of her thighs, pulling them up against her chest, so that her weight was all on Ben's cock. He was now nudging at the puckered opening, the slick head of his cock pressed against the tight entrance of her ass.

"Yes," Benjamin argued. "Let him feed...you ask him, he won't be able to say no. He's dying for the whole fucking feast a witch can offer him. Give it to him..."

Shadoe shuddered and screamed and begged, "Feed, Malachi." Desperate to feel everything he could offer her—that they could offer her—desperate to make them feel as good as they had made her feel.

Mal swore, brushing her hair away and striking, his teeth sinking in her neck, his mouth fastening on and drawing from her, sending hot lightning bolts coursing through her. At the same time, Ben's hands gripped the cheeks of her ass and pulled her open, and he pushed her down, driving her completely onto Malachi's cock.

The pain blistered her for a slow, agonizing second before exploding into a white-hot pleasure that arched her between their two bodies. Her body shuddered and writhed uncontrollably as she keened out Benjamin's name. He took her in a rough kiss, nipping at her lower lip, biting her tongue before sucking it greedily into his mouth.

A deep groan rumbled against her spine as Malachi pulled his mouth away, licking at the mark on her neck gently as he started to shaft her, his hands lifted her up before bringing her down so that their cocks were driven into her body together.

She shuddered and clenched around them as her orgasm continued to tear through her, the spasms slowly growing weaker, each one rocking through her, leaving an echo of it still coursing through her when the next one started.

It seemed to last for hours, yet no time at all. As she finally rode her orgasm through to the end, Malachi reached around to cup her breast, pinching the nipple between his thumb and forefinger, shifting his movements so that he and Benjamin fucked her body in tandem, one pulling out as the other drove in.

Her G-spot lit up as Benjamin shifted his stance, pushing her weight farther back against Malachi. Malachi wrapped his hands around her waist, supporting her weight against his chest, slowing his thrusts to gentle rocking motions, rolling his hips against her ass, the throbbing pulse of his cock teasing her mindlessly.

Under the caress of the plum-shaped head of his cock, hot and cold chills started to tear through her, splashes of fire hitting her belly. A whisper in a language she didn't know fell from Ben's lips, and his eyes flashed gold for a brief moment, then wind whipped through the air, coursing over her body, and then something caressed her clit.

She keened as the invisible touch started to vibrate against her clit, squeezing the air out of her lungs. Twin sensations focused on the tips of her breasts, plucking at the nipples, plumping them together like a pair of male hands. A harsh choking cry echoed through the room as the orgasm built in her belly.

"Not...yet," Malachi purred and she felt him sinking into her soul, into her mind, holding the climax just out of reach.

"What are you doing?" she sobbed, working her hips as best as she could, trying to come.

Malachi chuckled. "I could stroke you with my mind alone until you came—I can also hold you from it," he purred. "Let's let it last a while."

Benjamin laughed, cupping her ass in his hands, pulling the cheeks apart, stretching her more open for the slow, torturing glide of Malachi's cock. "He wants to drive you insane, sweet. I'm insane—you've done that to me, making me hot to see you fucked by him, making me want to have you eat my cock while he fucks you from behind. How have you done this?"

"Benjamin, please!"

She tightened her pussy around his cock, clenched her buttocks together, milking the hard columns of flesh. Benjamin swore and started to fuck her harder, wet sucking sounds filling the air, his cock ruddy, the flesh glistening with cream, breath sawing in and out of his hard, carved chest.

Malachi laughed shakily, seeking purchase on her body as he started to pump his cock into her ass with rough, quick digs. "It has lasted long enough, I think," he muttered. Gripping her hip with one hand, his other held firm on Benjamin's arm and Benjamin gripped Mal's arm so that they were locked together, her body connecting them as they pounded relentlessly inside her arching body.

Benjamin bellowed out her name as he started to come, his seed splashing inside her pussy. Malachi moaned against her neck as he followed, his cock jerking in the snug confines of her ass. "Sweet little fuck," Mal murmured, stroking his hand down her sides gently.

He pulled out gently, whispering against her neck, praising her, kissing her neck, her shoulders. She whimpered in pain as his semi-rigid cock left her ass, Benjamin still pulsating within her cleft. He sank to his knees and laid her on the ground, draping her thighs over his. "Look at me," Ben whispered hoarsely. "Say my name again, let me watch you…"

He stroked her slowly, his fingers teasing her clit. They never even noticed Mal leaving the room as they loved each other, slowly, sweetly this time. Benjamin worshipped her body with his eyes, his hands, his mouth as he rocked slowly within her.

"So pretty," he murmured as he bussed her lips with his, cruising over to her ear. "I love you."

He rocked within her, keeping his thrusts slow and gentle, even though the tightening of her pussy had him craving to plunge and ravage. He licked away the tears that seeped out of her eyes, and found his own eyes stinging, emotions unlike anything he had ever felt coursing through him.

"You are so wonderful, so amazing," he murmured against her mouth, the salt of her tears on his lips.

"Ben," she cried, arching her hips. She came with a long moan, feeling him climax inside her before his head fell to rest on her chest, pillowed between her breasts.

"I think I love you too," she said with a watery chuckle, wrapping her arms around his head, holding him against her as she ran her fingers through his thick silken hair. "I think I love you."

Chapter Ten

But late the following afternoon, after spending the rest of the night and late into the day with him, making love with him on the dining room table amid the remains of their breakfast, laughing when he smeared raspberry jam on her nipples and licked it off, she lay on the bed, with him sleeping behind her.

Reality started to intrude, and heat suffused her as she remembered what she had done.

She had fucked two men.

She had gloried in it, and she wanted it again.

What was going on with her? The monstrous lust wouldn't let her rest, and it was driving her insane. But she was thinking clearly now and her skin chilled, her mind filled with an incessant blathering that made no sense, meaningless words chasing one after the other without any understanding to them.

Slowly she slid from the bed, her feet soundless on the floor.

She dressed in complete silence, her eyes on Benjamin's sleeping body, praying he wouldn't wake. If he looked at her again, she'd fall back into the spell of the last fourteen hours.

Shadoe needed to think.

Needed to understand what had happened to her, what had taken her from quiet, shy Jillian to Shadoe, a shape-shifting witch who would fuck two men at once and crave more.

* * * * *

Marcus licked the inside of his cheek. The deep, inch-long gash had nearly closed. The healing a shape-shifter was capable of was amazing. That, combined with a special magicked tea he kept drinking nonstop had closed most of the cuts and lacerations on his body.

He was still bruised. Still battered. A few more days would wipe away all the marks of the beating he had taken at the hands of Benjamin Cross.

Cross.

That bastard Hunter had laid his hands on Marcus, had beaten him bloody, his greater strength pummeling Marcus into near submission. He would *never* admit how close he had come to throwing his head back and baring his throat to Cross, a sign of acknowledging Cross as Alpha.

No. It had been the mystical magick that clung to his skin.

Cross had done something, worked some bizarre magick only Hunters knew and made him feel fear. Something more than just the fear an Inherent could ooze.

And Cross would pay for it.

Marcus was going to take it out of his slut's hide. He had seen them, watching them through a pair of binoculars as he hid on the rolling hillside hundreds of yards away from her house, watching the curtains they hadn't closed as a vampire who walked in daylight fucked her pussy and that shape-shifting bastard Cross fucked her ass.

Marcus was going to get a piece of her ass, her hide, and her magick.

As she walked the streets with her head down, and her eyes unfocused, he waited in the house out in the boondocks, away from town, away from prying eyes, while his message was delivered.

In the corner, a small girl sobbed, crying noisily.

But she fell silent when Marcus lifted his head and stared at her, his eyes dark and raging with all the evils in hell.

* * * * *

Shadoe stared at the Inherent woman who stood in front of her, her chin lifted arrogantly, false bravado in her eyes.

In her hand, she held a note.

Shadoe jerked it and sneered at her, unaware of the wave of power that rolled from her, only glad when the stupid bitch's eyes shifted and then fell away.

A small golden braid fell out of the note when she unfolded it. With the amazing sense of smell that she still wasn't used to, she caught the hint of lotion and innocence, something forever associated with small children.

Want to be responsible for the death of a baby girl? Then ignore me and walk away.

M.

Her fingers clutched on the note, balling it into her fist as she lifted her blue eyes to the bitch in front of her. The remainder of the ballsy smile on her face fell away under the weight of Shadoe's angry, glowing eyes.

"Where is he?"

* * * * *

So now, she stood in the basement of a tiny house, miles outside of town, her eyes on Marcus' face, careful to keep from looking at the small girl. If she looked, she'd lose it. Fear was gnawing a hole in her belly as she faced down the man who had tried to rape her. Something dirty and slimy seemed to roll over her skin, clinging to her like a cloak that grew heavier the longer she was in there. It made her feel ill.

It was coming from him...his evil had fouled the very air around them. Her belly pitched and roiled as the fear and nausea warred side by side in her belly, along with a helpless, futile anger.

Part of her whispered that she could do this, that she could face Marcus...but the other part, the larger part that she worked to keep hidden, was almost stupefied, frozen with the fear that raged through her.

Licking her lips, she told herself...*It will be okay...you aren't who you used to be...* Now if she could just believe it.

First, she had to figure out how to get the pretty little child with the tear-stained face out of here.

"Who is she?" Shadoe asked flatly. "What do you want with her?"

Marcus grinned. "With her, not a damn thing. She's just a weak little human mongrel I found playing in her front yard. Her mother went to answer the phone, and there she was...small, sweet, innocent. I grabbed her. Fools like you are putty over a child like this. I knew I could get you to come to me. And now...we are going to finish what we started so many years ago."

"Let her go."

"And if I do?" he offered silkily. "What will I get?"

Dread curdled inside her, and even before she asked—she knew. "What do you want?"

"You. Here. For as long as I want. Doing whatever in the hell I tell you to. And if you try to run, I'll kill the next child I see. And if there's a mama around, I'll rape her while the kid watches." Marcus' words were flat, unemotional, and Shadoe saw the truth in his eyes.

"Are you insane?" she asked quietly. "I can't do that. I can't agree to *whatever*. For a bastard like you, that could mean becoming a murderer, a drug dealer, a million disgusting things that I refuse to do. I won't sell my soul to the devil, not even to save somebody from him."

Marcus chuckled. "Such an innocent little bitch you are. The Hunters would be proud to have you—but they won't want you when I'm done." He paused, a thoughtful look on his cold face. Then a smile lit his face and he offered, "If I give you my word that I won't force you to harm anybody, physically, mentally, emotionally...will you agree?"

"Whose opinion of harm are we going by?" she asked warily.

He grinned, revealing a charming, deceptive smile. "Yours, since I'm feeling so benevolent."

"And how do I know you'll honor your word?"

"I'll give you my blood oath. A witch can do deadly things when a blood oath is broken." Marcus cocked his head and said, "Time is wasting, Jillian Morgan. Will you run with me? Or let the kid die? And I'll make sure you watch."

"I won't run with you. But I'll stay here, doing whatever you ask, so long as I don't have to hurt anybody. That means, no drugs, no nasty spells, no murder. I'm going to take the bond," she said softly. *Even though I don't know what to do with it.* "If you break that bond, I'm going to take it out of your ass. But I'll do it, so long as you release the girl and don't try to take another. And I'm going into town with you when you take her back. Make sure she makes it back."

She'd find a way—fear be damned.

Marcus inclined his head. "So you can try to escape after I let her go? No. My bitch will take her into town."

Shadoe laughed, a chilly harsh sound that bounced off the walls in the basement. "Bullshit. You'll have her dispose of her like trash. If you want me, then we do it my way. I ride in the backseat with the little girl and we drop her off in front of her house. Once I see her in her mother's arms, we go and I'm all yours." As she said those final words, a memory loomed large...of him, holding her down and laughing at she fought and struggled.

Sick, sullen fear rocked her, but a baby... *God, how could You let him get his filthy hands on a baby?*

The small child, no more than three, snuffled in her sleep. Downy butter-colored curls tangled around her face as she slept, tiny little shudders racking her, as though she had cried herself to sleep not very long ago. Slitting her eyes, Shadoe said, "And if you think to touch her again, or anybody else in order to control me, think again. I'll kill you if you try."

Marcus snorted. "You? Kill me?"

Shadoe grinned, unaware her teeth had started to lengthen, a minor shape-shift that was a precursor to the complete change. She flashed a smile at him that felt wild, even to her. The woman cowered in the corner and whimpered. Marcus fell back a step before he realized what he had done. Then fury rippled through him and he rasped, "Bloody Hunters' magick. You can't kill me, bitch. You're too weak, too soft."

Shadoe cocked a brow. "I spent five years in prison because of you and a bastard like you. All the softness I had left after what you two did to me died in prison. I *can* kill you and I will enjoy it. Don't fuck with me."

* * * * *

Shadoe sat curled in the corner as the female shifter, Rachel, hauled the shivering child out of the car. "Hurt her, and I'll hurt you. You know I can," she said when Rachel carelessly let the girl's head thunk against the door when she leaned in to grab the shoe that had fallen off. Rachel stilled, then shifted the child from under her arm to cradling her against her chest, awkwardly, but much more gently.

"Don't threaten my bitch," Marcus growled.

Coldly, Shadoe said, "That wasn't part of the bargain. I'll threaten her if I want to. There's no reason for her to hurt the baby." Turning her face away, she drew a knee to her chest. Resting her chin on her knee, she watched Rachel set the girl on the sidewalk right by the house. The girl was kicking and struggling, sobbing for her mother, recognizing her home. As soon as her feet hit the ground, she took off running, stumbling, skinning her knee but back up again without blinking.

Rachel jumped back in and they sped off. "Damn it, I want to see her get to her mama," Shadoe snarled. "Stop the bloody car."

"So the bitch can give a vehicle description to the cops? You crazy or do you just think I'm stupid?" Marcus sneered.

"Both. This isn't the deal. Stop at the end of the street, jerk-off, or I'm gone. If you don't think I can...try me."

"Stupid bitch, do you think I'd just let that happen? Don't you realize I could easily go back there and grab that little whelp up? Kill her right in front of her mama, the cops... and *you*?" Marcus demanded, slamming on the brakes as he stared at her, his eyes wide with derision...and maybe something else?

"You do that, and you're going to attract attention you don't want," she said softly, thinking of Ben and Malachi. "I know all about the Hunters now, you know that. And I know you're afraid of them. You aren't going to do something that will attract too much of their attention. Of course, grabbing me is going to do that anyway...but you go on a slaughtering spree and I bet you won't live a week. They'll see to that. They are close to you now...you know that, and you're afraid, I can feel it."

Marcus growled, his eyes flashing at her in the mirror. The insidious fear that she had tried to shove aside reared its ugly head, but she only stared at him blankly, refusing to let him see it, afraid he'd see through her bravado.

It had worked, though, bravado or not. The car stopped. Shadoe craned her neck, watching as the child hit the front door just as it opened. A weary young woman with swollen eyes saw her, then snatched her up, cuddling her to her chest, eyes studying the street. Although Shadoe could see her with startling clarity, the woman couldn't possibly make out anything more than a vague color of the car as Marcus punched it.

Feeling his eyes on her as they slowed to a more sedate pace inside town, Shadoe lifted her head and met his eyes in the mirror. His malevolence washed over her and she lifted her chin, refusing to let him see the fear that was gnawing at her. With a dismissive glance, she turned her head away. Seconds later, her head crashed into the window as he hit her. "Don't you turn away from me, bitchling," he snarled, fury in his eyes.

Her hair hung in her eyes, and she tasted the blood in her mouth where her inner cheek had split under his blow. Under that blow, her fear started to shift, mixing with the helpless anger, and hatred. The hatred gave her purpose... Hatred was good, much better than that blinding fear she had been living with until just this second.

Narrowing her eyes, she met his gaze in the mirror and held it, her hatred oozing from her pores. She held his gaze and watched as the arrogance started to fade—she held it until his eyes fell away.

Then she settled down and looped her arm around her knee. It was time to plan.

With a bone-deep knowledge, she knew she could outrun him, outwit him, escape and melt into the background as he searched for her. Outwit, outrun...hide, she could do that, she was certain.

What she wasn't so certain about was killing him—no matter how bravely she made herself act as she faced him down. And if she escaped, it would leave him free to finish the promise he had made, and that wasn't to be allowed.

He would have to die, and if that meant she would had to try to kill him, then so be it.

Of course, I can always hope Ben beats me to it, she thought sardonically.

* * * * *

When he woke up alone, Benjamin had a gut-deep feeling that something was wrong.

The bed next to him was cold, and Shadoe wasn't in the house. He couldn't smell the soft fragrance of her skin, nor could he hear the telltale beating of her heart.

Rising, he paced the small room, uneasy, as time passed.

He had pushed too much on her lately, made her accept too much.

And some things that many people never even thought of in the context of stories.

When he finally wandered out of his room, he resumed his pacing in the living room. His hair was disarrayed from all the times he had run his hands through it, and his scowl grew darker and darker as more time passed.

Finally, after four hours of her not walking through the door, his patience snapped. Stalking to the bathroom, he grabbed a comb.

Not a damn hair on it.

Not one strand on the sink.

Not on the towel, nor in the shower drain.

All that long, thick hair and not one bloody strand.

He stepped on top of the toilet and looked on top of the shelving unit, his eyes gleaming when he saw the brush sitting there amid a light film of dust, a few hair bands, and a box of tampons.

A few strands were woven through the rough bristles. Gently, he tugged them free and smoothed them straight before he laid the strands in his cupped palm. Heat flooded the room, centered over his palm, gaining in strength, light starting to swirl.

When the golden ball lifted from his palm, it glowed translucent as it spun. But it wasn't Shadoe's face it showed. It was a child's, tear-stained, peaceful in sleep. As Benjamin watched, a woman's hand stroked over the sleeping child's cheek and the focus shifted.

Now he was watching from a point beyond the girl's shoulder and he could see a woman, the woman who had been caressing the girl's cheek. Her mama, most likely. The facial structure was the same and both had a rather unique shade of hair, true platinum blonde and thick with curls.

Her mouth opened but Ben knew he'd hear no sounds.

However, he did see something almost as enlightening. Two policemen.

The mother gestured wildly, her eyes tear-filled, frustration in every line of her face, every move of her body.

The cops exchanged glances as the woman lowered her head into her hands and started to sob. The younger one moved over and sat down beside her, rubbing her shoulder, making gentle hushing sounds by the looks of it. After a moment, she calmed and the cop moved his hands, spread them wide as if to say, *help me out here...*

Pulling a notebook out of his pocket, he listened and nodded, jotting down a few more notes as the woman spoke.

Benjamin saw some of the scrawl. And a growl trickled loose as he read *pretty lady with "glowy" eyes.*

He would kill Marcus.

Benjamin raced on, keeping to the outskirts of town. He couldn't find her scent.

Damnation, why couldn't he find her?

It was almost as if something had erased her scent. A town of less than five hundred, she was *here* somewhere. But even if she had been taken out of town, he should still be able to catch the scent from her presence over the past few days.

But the whole damn town was wiped clean.

Even her own home.

* * * * *

Shadoe watched through the vision orb Benjamin had been teaching her to use. It hovered above her palm and she felt tears sting her eyes as it tracked Ben's dark furry hide as he ran in wolf form throughout town, pausing from time to time to lift his head and scent the air.

Her scent was nowhere to be found.

Marcus had told her to wipe the town clean of it, and when she had said she didn't know how, he had backhanded her again. Tonguing her lip, she winced as the pain bloomed afresh in her busted lip.

After that, he ignored her, taking his bitch to his room, and she could hear them as they fucked. Marcus made damn sure of that, leaving her in the room right next door, leaving the door open.

He was going to pay for this. Holy hell was he going to pay.

An hour later, he shoved the woman out of his room, and Shadoe winced at the look on Rachel's face, like that of a puppy dog, full of worship and the desire to please...and shame.

She saw Shadoe looking at her and tossed her hair, trying vainly to give a pleased smile—but she failed and her face crumpled. As she whirled and left the room, still naked, Shadoe felt the smallest trickle of pity well in her.

"Get your skinny ass moving and stop moping around," Marcus growled as he stalked into the room. "You placed yourself in my hands. Be mad at yourself for being such a weak little bitch."

The ball he couldn't see glimmered out, fading away, leaving darting sparkles lingering in its place. "What in the hell do you want?"

Marcus smiled. A nasty, evil smile. "I've never had a witch under my hands before. You are going to come in very handy. Starting now." He started to pace around her in a slow circle as he continued, "The banks in town... You can use your magick to slide in and out without the cameras seeing you. I know quite a bit about witches. When you unleash a burst of power, it tends to fry the more complex equipment, cameras, security alarms, motion sensors... You're going to go into the Grand National Bank and relieve them of some of their money."

"I never agreed to become a thief," she ground out.

"Ah, but you did. Whatever I want, so long as it doesn't harm another. This won't harm anybody. So get ready," he ordered, trailing one hand down her face, her neck, circling his finger around her nipple.

Her skin started to crawl.

But she couldn't figure out if it was from his touch or the fact that she was going to break the law.

Jerking back, she said, "If I have to break the law, then I need to concentrate. I can't do it with you touching me." The bravado was pretty impressive, even with the trembling voice.

Firm up, Shadoe... Jillian would be trembling and incoherent with fear. You're more than that now. Angling her chin, she held firm when he moved closer, close enough for her to feel his body heat. Her skin crawled. Disgust and nausea roiled through her, yet she kept her face impassive when he moved close enough for her to feel the rock-hard, furnace-like heat of his body, then the pulse of his cock through his trousers.

He was horny.

Turned on like never before. All over terrorizing her, threatening her. His eyes narrowed as she failed to react to his threatening body language. "You went and grew some balls, didn't you? What did that bastard lead you to believe, Jillian? You aren't invincible. You're less than nothing, *nothing*."

At his words, she felt the anger inside expand until it eclipsed everything else...even the fear that had held her almost numb.

Nothing? she thought, enraged. *I'll show him nothing.* Lifting her hand, she couldn't stop the small, cool smile that spread over her lips as heat flared from her hand and jumped from her to him, knocking him ten feet back, scalding his flesh, singeing his clothes. "Nothing?" she asked coldly.

Like most shape-shifters, Marcus had a deadly fear of fire. Fire was one of the few things that could kill him. Eyes wide with panic, he pounded at his chest as he swore and Shadoe laughed. "You're not on fire, idiot," she said, turning around and sauntering away. "But I will remember how much it scared you."

Damn it, he was...just pathetic, she realized. Why hadn't she seen that before?

"Bitch!" Marcus seethed, his shirt hanging in charred tatters around his shoulders, his chest beneath red and blistering. He started to charge her and Shadoe whipped around, flinging her hand out. The words whispered into her as though from somewhere else, bringing her a knowledge she hadn't before known.

"*Incindiaire*," she whispered, the unfamiliar word falling awkwardly from her lips.

When a ring of fire surrounded her, separating her from Marcus, she yelped instinctively. Wide-eyed, she stared around her at the barrier of fire. "Sweet heaven," she murmured. Then, unable to stop the cocky smile on her face, she met the shape-shifter's eyes insolently.

In his eyes, she saw the knowledge that maybe he had bitten off more than he could chew.

And Shadoe finally started to realize it, as well. He was weaker than she was… As that knowledge flooded her, she lifted her head, staring at him squarely, feeling the chains of fear that had bound her slowly flow away. Holding out her hand, she let it hover above the flames for a moment, before lowering it, palm down to the ground. As her hand moved, the flames died down until they winked out completely. Facing Marcus, she said softly, "The scared little girl you went after years ago is gone, Marcus. Deal with it."

* * * * *

The fear in his belly made him mean.

He wanted to strike out, to hurt, to maim. But the one he wanted to hurt the most seemed to be out of his reach. For now.

The knowledge that she was so much more than he had thought hovered in the back of his mind. Refusing to acknowledge it before now had kept him from having to acknowledge that he had been wrong when he'd thought Benjamin and the Hunter vampire were the ones with the power.

No. He couldn't deal with her.

But he knew who could. Abandoning the plans for breaking into the bank, he focused instead on making calls. The rogue pack he had once run with was gone, annihilated by the damned Hunters. But there were a few others who would know how to contact him.

Dumas was only spoken of in soft, hushed whispers. Too many people feared him. He moved around like a Gypsy and was harder to track than dust in the wind.

But where there was a will, Marcus told himself.

Finally, by the end of the day, he had something. Not a location, but a contact. And the possibility of money — in exchange for a Hunter's bitch.

"Fuck the bank, I have a better idea," he announced to the small group of people.

Jillian was still on the couch where she had been sitting since earlier that morning. The food he had ordered Rachel to fix for her sat untouched. Narrowing his eyes, he said, "You haven't eaten. Not once since you came down here."

"So sorry. The sight of you all makes me lose my appetite... I may never be able to eat again," she drawled. Her eyes were cold, disdainful.

He wanted to see them bright with fear again. With terror.

The few times fear had broken through with her, she had smashed it. She was laughing at him, silently, mockingly. "Eat the damn food — that's an order, bitch, otherwise I go grab me a snack," he spat, shooting across the room and bending over her, fisting his hand in her hair.

Something moved in her eyes for the briefest of seconds. "I am not hungry," she said, slowly enunciating as though speaking to an imbecile.

"Hungry or not, eat the damn food. I know using magick will make you burn off your reserves and you have to replenish them. If you think to kill yourself through starvation...*think twice*. I will make you regret that choice, bitch, believe me."

Marcus lifted his lip in a cold smile as she reached for the sandwich, her eyes shining with hate.

"Good bitch," he whispered into her ear before releasing her hair.

Turning his eyes to the werewolves, he ignored Jillian as she slowly ate. "We're heading out, going to find us some fresh hunting ground. Be ready to leave as soon as I tell you," he said, grinning wildly.

Soon…

* * * * *

Malachi grimaced as Benjamin plowed his fist into a wall.

Two days.

It had been two days since she had disappeared and there was no fucking sign of her, of Marcus, or the remaining wolves of the old pack. She had disappeared without so much as a fucking trace and Benjamin had pushed himself to his limits, but without success.

"Call for help," Malachi finally said, his voice quiet. "You need a witch who is closer to her level. Then maybe we can find her. You're good, Cross. But she is phenomenal. We need a phenomenal witch to locate her, to power past the roadblocks she has thrown up."

"Where is she? Why did she hide herself, damn it? Bloody fuck, how did she know *how* to hide herself?" Benjamin snarled, whipping around and staring at Malachi across the room.

The muscles in Cross' face were rippling, and his eyes glittered red with his rage. Malachi had to tamp down his own instinctive emotions that rose in response to such fury.

"She had no choice. Or at least Marcus convinced her of that," Malachi answered simply. "She's young, and not a true, trained Hunter either. She doesna know that all she had to do was whisper his name to us and he was dead. Chances are, boy, he threatened another child. Offered to release the one he had, and leave others alone in return for her *good* behavior. He is a lying sack of shit, yet she may not realize how pathetic, how easily beaten one like him is."

"*She* could kill him," Benjamin snapped, plowing a hand through his hair. "With just a damn thought, she could end his life. With *one touch* she could kill him."

Malachi said softly, "I don't think she's realized that yet. 'Tis a tremendous power, that. And just a month ago, she was living the life of a mortal." He pushed away from the wall and walked over to Cross, the long coat he had shrugged into flapping around his ankles. His heavy mane of hair was woven into a tight braid and hanging over one broad shoulder in a fiery rope. Catching Ben's arm, he brought the wolf to a halt and waited until that flashing, heated gaze met his. "Call for help. Ya need another witch, Cross. Do it. *Now*. Before it's too late. Marcus will learn, verra soon, if he hasna already. He canna control her. So he will give her to somebody who can."

Chapter Eleven

Malachi stood in the corner, a silent, foreboding figure, as Benjamin trailed a wet hand down a mirror, speaking in some language Malachi suspected only the witches of the Council knew.

He had seen this done enough to know that Benjamin was placing a summons to another witch. If she was by chance near any reflective surface, she'd feel the summons and touch her hand to the surface and her face would waver into view. If she wasn't, then a bell would echo the moment she neared, summoning Benjamin.

Who will he call?

Kelsey? Most likely. Sarel and Lori were powerful things, but Cross would go straight for the most powerful for his woman, one who had all the knowledge age could provide. At least, that was Malachi's theory. He might even summon Agnes, although she was so very ancient, even for a witch, that she'd not be leaving her native England for anything short of the final battles.

But the face that slowly came into view wasn't one that Malachi had been expecting.

Leandra.

From what he could tell, she was in Excelsior. A slow smile spread across Malachi's face.

Bloody hell. She had done it.

Her eyes met his briefly, and he felt something, a pride he rarely allowed himself, pride in doing something momentous, as she gave him a slow nod. In her eyes, he saw the beginnings of self-acceptance.

Which meant she was forgiving herself.

"What ya wanting wit' me, Cross?" she asked curiously. One black brow winged up and she cocked her head.

"Your help," Benjamin said levelly. His eyes flickered as he looked past her shoulder and saw where she was, the library, unmistakable, vast, full of things of power that were better left alone. "You are at Excelsior."

She inclined her head. "Somebody opened me eyes." She glanced around her with blank eyes, but when she looked back at them, both of them could sense the awe that filled her. "I was gettin' ready to leave, even though dat bastard Malachi had said tings dat made me head spin as I tried to take it in. I was leavin'. And dey stopped me. I thought at first dey were going to do what I've been waiting on for years. I thought I was dead. And I was relieved dat it was over," she murmured.

"But dey didn't want me dead. Agnes was wit' dem — she left England for me." Chuckling, she met Ben's eyes. "Dey be afraid of me, many of dem. Just like you said. But not her." Something entered her eyes that Malachi suspected was very foreign. Love, for that old woman. "Not her. She tell me that it is time I face meself. Because I can never be what I was meant to be until I can let go of me own anger. 'Face yourself', she told me. 'And be free.'"

Wonder suffused her voice and she whispered, "I've never been free. Until now."

A grin spread across her face and she wagged a finger at Benjamin. "Ya knew what would happen if I got here, ya bastard. Ya knew." Bowing her head, she murmured, "Thank you."

The moment passed then, and her old arrogance returned. Crossing her arms over her chest, she said, "Ya keep summoning me like dis, Cross. What ya want from me dis time?"

The amazing thing about a flier, Benjamin mused, you could speak with them from thousands of miles away one moment, and then be facing them in the next.

He hadn't even had time to finish explaining when she pressed her hand to the mirror, canceling the spell. He was growling, furious, and ready to blast her when the air around him tightened.

She was standing in front of him five seconds later, a pack in one hand, and an apple in the other. She crunched into the shiny red fruit and chewed as she met his eyes.

After swallowing, she lifted the apple for a second bite, but first she said, "Ya could have gotten any witch ya wanted here. Why me?"

"Because you can fight. I want a warrior as well as a scholar. Only a few of us fit that bill, Leandra," he said.

She ate more of the apple, insolence written in every line of her body, all over her exotic face.

Malachi laughed. "She has got to be the cockiest bitch I've ever met. Damn it, I like you, Leandra," he said, shaking his head.

She arched a brow and turned away, but not before they both glimpsed the flush on her face.

Poor kid. The thought came abruptly to Ben's mind as he watched her walk away, looking anywhere but at them. How rough must it have been for her? How much of an outcast did she feel if such simple words embarrassed her?

But he forgot the momentary distraction when Leandra lifted a book that Shadoe had been flipping through for the past few weeks. Her eyes closed and her head fell back.

"You can't track her scent. I've already tried. She erased her touch, her scent from everything," Benjamin said quietly.

"Not from her—I can feel her. A soul like mine," she whispered. "I recognized that the moment we saw each other. And so did she." Her eyes opened, and something odd passed through them, almost eagerness, wonder. "A soul like mine... Surrounded by evil."

Then her face drew tight with strain, and rage made her eyes start to gleam. She said, "De man wit' her is taking her to

Louisiana. Dere's a man dere he plans on giving Shadoe to. He wants her broken, and he can't do it, dat weak bastard."

Fury flooded Benjamin, and with it, the primal power of the Wolf, straining inside his skin, yearning to be free and to start the Hunt. His muscles spasmed and skin rippled like water — he fought it back.

"We leave now," he said quietly. "Nobody touches what is mine." The setting sun was shining through the cracks in the blinds, true dark still an hour away. Casting the streams of light a glance, he told Malachi, "I'm assuming you'll have no trouble catching up with us?"

Malachi grinned. "Weeelll, if I let ye leave without me, I'd catch up easy enough. But there's no need for me to linger here." His face went blank as he spoke, and Benjamin bit down the questions that rose. But he understood well enough what the vampire didn't say. The sun was very little, if any, deterrent to him.

Hell, were all the tales he'd heard of Malachi true? Of course, if they were, that made him an even more powerful ally than Benjamin had expected.

But it occurred to Ben — what if they ever ran into a vampire that was Malachi's equal? And he was on the wrong side.

* * * * *

Leandra couldn't get over watching a vampire walk in the daylight.

She'd heard of Torrance O'Reilly, now known as Torrance Donovan. The Huntress was supposed to be only legend, a young vampire who could blend in with the mortals, one who had all of the vampires' strengths, none of their weaknesses.

But Malachi wasn't of her ilk. He was pure vampire, and as he flipped on a pair of shades, covering eyes that squinted at the sunlight, she suspected he had many of their weaknesses. He just had a higher tolerance. One that was probably close to immeasurable.

Her skin buzzed just being close to him. Everything about her felt pushed to the maximum of sensation, from the buzzing of her skin, the tightening of her nipples, the hot little flashes that hit her belly every time he turned those midnight blue eyes her way.

His eyes, his hands, everything inside of him, everything that made him Malachi, had the power to draw.

Yet, as she slid back behind her shields, it faded, dying down, until looking at him was like looking at the ancient works of art she had seen in Milan. Awe-inspiring, but not for her.

Of course, she did have to admit a bit of envy for the woman that man was meant for.

She folded her long legs up as she climbed into the SUV, leaving the front seat for the vamp and the Inherent. With a wry grin, she wondered if SUVs had become the mode of transportation for the paranormal population by choice or by chance. How many SUVs had she ridden in since she had fallen in with those she used to hunt? Cross had driven one, Kelsey, three of the Hunters who had tagged her in New Mexico…

And Mike…he'd driven one.

Clenching her jaw, she ordered herself *not* to think of him. That one would be her undoing.

Settling down, she closed her eyes and focused once more on the other woman. That done, the thoughts of the man she had damn near killed faded. For the moment.

Cradling the book in her hands, she murmured, "We're coming, girl. We're coming."

* * * * *

Shadoe was in trouble.

She knew it the moment she stepped through the door of the isolated monolith on the outskirts of Baton Rogue. The trees damn near hid the thing from view. And some ancient magick hid it from the senses. She could feel those spells part around her as Marcus drove, following the pathway that was leading her to her doom, for certain.

Nobody would know this place was here, unless they already knew of its existence.

Lost in a forest of cypress trees and grand oaks, the front lawn dotted with magnolia trees that filled the air with a sweet perfume, it was an isolated world from an era long gone.

It was lit by candlelight and magick.

As she followed Marcus down the hall, she could feel the weight of that magick pressing in on her, testing her.

And eyes. She could feel eyes on her, eager to discover her secrets. Swallowing her fear, she took stock, reaching out the way Benjamin had showed her.

Only to be flung back, as though an unseen hand struck her across the face, she went flying.

Her head struck the wall and she crumpled, unconscious, to the ground.

"Fuck, Pierre, was that necessary?" Marcus growled, as he turned and watched Jillian hit the ground.

"You should have told your bitch to keep her hands to herself," a soft, accented voice murmured.

Out of the shadows he came, a slimly built man with gilt-colored hair falling to his ass in loose waves.

"She's not my bitch," Marcus said with a tiny grin. "I'd planned on selling her to you."

Pierre gave the crumpled body a negligent glance and said, "Why should I want her?"

"Because she belongs to the Hunters," Marcus replied easily.

When Pierre's grass green eyes lit with interest, Marcus almost rubbed his hands together in satisfaction.

He had him. Oh yes…he had him.

* * * * *

As he followed the naked ass of one of Pierre's slaves into the formal dining room, he took stock, eyeing a huddled body in the corner with hunger.

"Have her, if you like," Pierre said. "I have something much more appetizing to look forward to now." He moved his eyes to the ceiling. Above him, his new toy was being stripped and bathed clean of the scents of the men she had been fucking, and clean of the scents that had soaked into her pores while she had been with Marcus.

Pierre Dumas could smell the scent of a wolf. Inherent, he was fairly certain. And there had been another scent, faint, but oddly familiar.

Pierre wasn't sure what that one was.

Not that it mattered. She belonged to him now.

And the Hunters didn't even know he existed.

His magick took care of that. Wiping his touch clean every time he moved on, choosing his prey wisely, he had eluded the eyes of the Hunters for five centuries.

It was an amusing game to him, a game of chess they didn't even know they were playing.

But Pierre had grown tired, of late, of playing in the shadows.

And too many of the vamps he had sired were dying by the wayside. None had managed to find their way into the esteemed Council. And he had sired many, hoping for just that.

Offspring of his inside the Council meant *he* was inside the Council. He could slide inside the mind and never leave any trace of his passing. None of the others he had ever touched had remembered. They didn't even remember his face after they had been sired, couldn't recall the specifics of anything.

And he liked it that way.

Operating in the dark gave him freedom. Made it easier to hunt without being "Hunted".

Although a select few did know of him.

Men like Marcus, who could be of value to him.

Pierre smiled at the woman who knelt between his thighs. Her lips were wrapped around his cock, sliding up and down with practiced moves, a smile dancing in her eyes.

By the corner of one of her lids, a tattoo winked.

* * * * *

Leandra said, "She be inside a house, but I cannot read her. She was there one moment, den gone de next, like a wall came down."

Behind that wall, something ancient lurked. She sensed the great power, the great age.

Benjamin blew out a breath and asked, "If we drive around, do you think you'll be able to pick anything up?"

Leandra lifted one shoulder. She didn't like this. She felt blind...too blind. Something odd was going on and she didn't know how to handle it. The gifts she had alternately cursed and relied upon throughout her life didn't seem to be working right now. As though something was blocking her.

Malachi frowned. "Something is blocking you," he murmured, ignoring the dumb look on her face when her jaw dropped open.

A mindreader...he can read my damn mind? She knew vampires could skim through the thoughts of mortals, but damn it, she wasn't a mortal, it shouldn't be that bloody easy.

He cast a glance. "It's not as easy as all that, unless you go broadcasting your thoughts like you just did, pet. The words were on your face, in your eyes. I didn't have to read a bloody thing," he said, quirking a brow. "Until you went and shouted just now, *a mindreader...* I hadn't ever breached your mental walls. Not that I had tried."

Her cheeks flushed but her dismay faded as Malachi started to...hell, she didn't know how to describe what she was seeing. He just suddenly became *more*, his eyes glowing as though lit from within, his fangs dropping, and he even seemed larger, as though he was looming over her and Benjamin. Power rippled from him, the power of his very presence, stumping her into momentary silence.

It was having a similar effect on Benjamin and the shifter didn't like it. She had to fight the urge to throw herself at his feet, although there might be some interesting things to do while down there. Benjamin, on the other hand, wouldn't find anything worthwhile in submitting to the ancient one and the urges rolling through him were making him uneasy, restless, enough that she could see wildness swirling in his eyes as the wolf within him started to wake.

"There's something here that shouldn't be... Where is the closest Hunter? Is it a vamp? A wolf pack?"

Benjamin slowly said, "There's a pack on the other side of New Orleans. A vamp at the border. Eli commented that it's not a good idea to have too many of our kind around here. Too many people seem to look for us here, even though most of humanity doesn't even believe in us. We have to keep a low profile in this sort of place. But a few members from the pack are full Hunters and they live within the city."

"Any witches? No vampires closer than the border?"

Benjamin frowned. "Nobody wants any territory here. The pack is several hundred years old, one of the oldest in the country, but once several of the pack members were recruited by the Council, nobody ever felt the desire to settle here. The few kids we take from here that are inclined to become Hunters don't want to come back. It's watched, order is maintained."

"Is it really?" Malachi mused. Shaking his head, he said, "There is something here that shouldn't be. A blackness, a cloud..."

"There's nothing here, Mal. I don't sense a damn thing," Benjamin said, brushing it aside. "We need to get moving and find Shadoe."

Leandra shivered, as something raced down her spine at Malachi's words. But she forgot her unease within the hour.

And as they drove, Benjamin grew more agitated. Shifting in his seat, slapping one broad hand against a muscled thigh, his eyes darting over the buildings and the people with a blankness that made her worry.

But as a long, powerfully built sax player on the street corner caught her eye, she forgot even her worry.

And why they were there.

* * * * *

Malachi felt cold dread settle in him as Benjamin tossed him an aggressive, challenging glance.

Bloody hell there wasn't something there.

Benjamin had just circled the same block three times and was now parked at the side of the street, his eyes locked on the slender ebony-skinned woman who was dancing at the side of the sax player.

The heat had both the witch and the shape-shifter sweating lightly, the evening breeze that floated through the open windows doing little to cool them.

It didn't affect Malachi—under normal circumstances, he would have enjoyed the scent of *life* that was hovering just outside the black SUV.

However, this wasn't normal. Something was wrong…very, very wrong.

"How is staring at that pretty thing helping you find Shadoe?"

Benjamin tossed a disinterested glance as he reached for the door. "Who?"

Bloody hell…

Malachi was slow to move as he assimilated that response. The blankness in Benjamin's gaze, the restlessness and loss of purpose now written in his eyes. He turned his head to speak softly to Leandra, only to see her sliding to the edge of the seat, her amber eyes locked on the bald, powerfully built white man who was playing the sax, the sleek, ebony beauty pressed up against his back, her hands on his hips as they danced for their audience.

"Leandra," Malachi whispered, dropping his shielding a bit.

He saw her response in the way she licked her lips, how her nipples stiffened under the confines of her shirt and bra. Cocking her head, she stared at him with a puzzled look on her face. "Ummm," she purred, shifting forward and resting her cheek on the side of Benjamin's seat, her eyes locked on Mal's face.

"Isn't there something you're supposed to be doing?" he asked quietly.

"Besides going over dere and getting dat man away from his horn long enough to fuck me?" she asked, grinning cheekily.

Oh, that decides it, something is definitely not right. Shaking his head, Malachi leaned closer until they were nose to nose. "Wake up, witchling... Something isn't right. You came here to *do* something. What was it?"

Her eyes clouded and she frowned. "I'd rather be over dere with him. I'd rather do *him* den whatever it was," she drawled, but he could see the confusion in her eyes. Canting her head to the side, she worried her lip with her teeth. "I don't know...looking. I was looking for something. For—somebody."

"Aye, you were." He waited.

"A woman." A shudder racked her body and her hands shot up, plowing through her braids, clutching them in her hands. "I can't tink. What is wrong wit' me?"

"A verra powerful spell. Och...I kin feel it, pounding at my mind, like waves against the sand." He could feel it, battering, trying to get inside his mind, but he was far too old, far too powerful for something as meager as a spell to break into his mind.

Leandra and Ben on the other hand...it had gotten to them.

Leandra's eyes were starting to glow now, Mal observed. Reaching out, he laid a hand on her skin and dropped his shields, watching as her body arched up and a startled gasp fell from her lips. Her eyes glowed hot and hungry and then she started to swear.

"Fucking vampire, what are ya doin'?" she snapped, jerking away and flinging herself against the back of the seat, lust rolling from her in waves. Her nipples were hard and peaked, swelling against the front of the plain black T-shirt she wore, and he could smell the cream gathering in her pussy. His own cock jerked in response and he felt like swearing in return.

But her eyes were clear.

"Are ye aware now, witchling?" he asked, already knowing the answer.

"Damn straight I'm aware, ya bastard. What were ya tinkin'?" she snarled. Then her face cleared and her eyes went cold as that awareness trickled through, bringing with it memory. Her eyes moved to the sax player and she licked her lips, a nervous reaction as she tried to move her mind around what had damn near overtaken her. "What in de holy hell was dat?"

"A spell, verra powerful," he reiterated. "It's heavier than a rain cloud, hanging over the whole bloody city and catching everybody inside within its net."

"How...how can dat be possible?" she asked, her voice faint. "Dat would take so much energy, so much strength...de witch would have to be more than ancient to have built up enough energy to lay the spell, and keep it up all de time. It would take the power of centuries to create and maintain. Witches don't live dat long."

"Not unless they've bonded with vampire or an Inherent, no. The bond would let her live as long as her mate's normal lifespan. But if that is the case—" his words fell off ominously as the light in his eyes started to pulse with rage. "Why haven't the wolves in the pack made us aware?"

"If it's dat powerful, they may have fallen prey to it as well," Leandra whispered, swallowing the knot of fear in her throat, her eyes moving away from Malachi's.

"Aye. They do whatever Hunting this witch lets them do to keep them thinking they are doin' their bloody job," he growled, his fangs aching and throbbing, his eyes incandescent in his anger. "Just enough, and no more."

His rage was rolling from him in overpowering waves and he saw the reaction it was causing in her. He could see her nervousness as she moved her eyes away to keep him from seeing the angry spark his rage unwillingly lit within her. Could see it in the way she carefully inched back, all moves made in the least threatening way possible. She knew how to avoid rousing a dominant monster's anger, knew how to avoid setting off any kind of confrontation, even when it sparked her own anger.

Swallowing it down, banking it, he said softly, "Be easy, Leandra. We need to get Cross."

Benjamin had seduced the dancer into leaving the sax player and he had her currently backed up against an ivy-covered fence, leaning into her, sexual interest written in every line of his body. As he lowered his mouth to whisper in her ear, he skimmed one hand down her side, the heel of his hand stroking the outer curve of her breast.

Her eyes were hot, almost drugged.

"Bleeding hell," Malachi swore. "He's pulling her in."

Leandra cocked a brow.

"You've been around Inherents long enough to know they can leak fear almost as well as a vampire, they can inspire it, cause it whenever they want in a lesser being. Somebody whose will isn't as strong as his own…you know this?"

She cocked her head, waiting.

"They can do the same with lust. An Inherent can be the most seductive creature you'll ever meet—it's in their nature,"

Malachi said, climbing from the car, Leandra at his back. "And he's not bothering to hide any of his nature from her."

"So I see," Leandra murmured, angling her head and licking her lips as Benjamin slid his hand inside the dancer's form-fitting shirt, pushing dangerously close to one firm, jutting breast.

"Fuck me, if he has five more minutes, he'll be fucking her on the street and then we'll have to get him out of jail," Malachi snapped, striding forward.

"Cross," he said, leaning his mouth down and rasping the word in the shifter's ear.

"Get the fuck away, buddy," Benjamin said, jamming his elbow back into Mal's stomach. His hand was cupping her breast now, and from the look of it, his fingers were tugging the nipple. The woman was limp and already nearly mad with hunger.

Malachi could smell it on her, and smell Benjamin's rising lust. The sharp pain in his belly faded quickly and Malachi thought it was a damn good thing that a cop hadn't seen this display and gotten to them. If Benjamin had jabbed that elbow at a mortal and not a vampire, it would have done internal damage just from the force of the blow.

"You aren't here to get laid," Malachi said flatly as he reached out and jerked Benjamin's head back simply by grabbing a handful of hair and pulling.

Benjamin let the woman go as he jerked free, whirling on Malachi and tensing to lunge.

"Cross…"

Malachi tensed as Leandra's voice rolled over them, soft and seductive. She swayed between them, her hips rolling seductively, her nipples hard and pebbled under her shirt. Malachi started to swear, but then the gleam in her eyes had him relaxing.

Damn it, this was getting annoying as hell.

The woman was staring at Leandra with rage in her eyes, because Benjamin was now circling around Leandra like a caged animal, full of hunger, full of lust. His cock was swelling against the fly of his jeans and his eyes were glowing. And they were attracting far too much attention.

Benjamin jerked her up against him, fisting one hand in the thick, dark dense braids, lowering his head. The other hand he kept on her hip, holding her firmly against his groin as he rocked his hips into hers.

She smiled seductively as she reached up and laid one hand against his cheek.

Malachi felt the swell of power ripple through the air, and he watched with awe as she broke through the other spell, not with power, but with stealth, a woman's weapons, sliding under the spell that clouded his mind, and slipping into his heart. "Does my body feel as good to you as Shadoe's?" she purred.

Benjamin froze. "Shadoe..." he murmured, his mouth just a breath away from hers.

"Hmmm... ya know, dat pretty witch you came here to find?" she offered, smiling sweetly.

Malachi surmised, as the comprehension started to dawn on him, that all it took for the spell to shatter was to acknowledge it, to push against it. Benjamin jerked back from Leandra as though she was contaminated, but she only laughed.

"My guess is dat I don't compare," she chuckled. Running her red tongue across her bottom lip, she added impishly, "Too bad."

As people around them started to murmur, and the dancer pushed closer, aiming for Leandra, she said, "I tink we need t' be going."

Benjamin was already back in the SUV, his face drawn tight and pale with fury, his eyes glittering. "Nobody fucking messes with my head," he muttered, jamming the key in, and gunning the gas.

Leandra and Malachi tumbled in only moments before he shot away from the curb, still swearing.

"Well...de good news is dat I can tink a little clearer," Leandra said blandly. "And you're heading in da wrong direction. Shadoe is on the other side of town."

* * * * *

Benjamin had never been so furious. Although embarrassment warred a close second.

Something had sneaked inside his head and stolen a part of him, seducing him into forgetting.

And to try to make him forget Shadoe...oh, somebody was going to pay for that. He'd turn them into a talking carpet for that, flay their skin from their bodies, laughing all the while.

He still couldn't feel her.

But Leandra could sense her, somehow.

She was powerful, more so than Benjamin. And for that, he thanked God.

They were outside town now, driving down a narrow, overgrown street that was more of a path than a road. Finally, she pointed to a smaller path and said, "Pull in dere. Dere's nothing down dat way and we can walk the rest of de way."

"Walk?" Benjamin growled.

"Yes, walk. We have to figure out what we are dealin' with," she said quietly. "It's something...different."

Chapter Twelve

Shadoe's eyes opened.

She lay on her side, surrounded by silk and lace. Naked.

She had never been so afraid in her life. Not when she had been pinned under Jimmy's body, not when she had driven a blade into Marcus to keep him from raping her, not even when she had seen Marcus shift to wolven form that first time as she had burned Jimmy's heart to ash with her touch.

Something insidious was inside her mind. Blackness was trying to eat away at her.

"Not yet...but I shall," a soft voice purred from over her shoulder.

She bit back the scream that rose to her lips and rolled limply onto her back when a cool hand tugged her over. He had read her mind.

"*Oui*. And such a tasty treat you are going to be, Shadoe, child of the Hunters," he mused, lowering his head to sniff at her skin.

"I'm not a fucking treat," she said, forcing confidence into her voice. Even though she wanted nothing more than to babble incoherently with fear.

He laughed and the sound rolled over her like silk. He traced a finger around her soft nipple and she cowered against the mattress, his touch feeling dirty and foul. Her skin shrank tight at his cold touch and she wanted to rail against her body's reaction, at what looked to be arousal. "You are...and such a sweet, innocent thing you are. I can hardly wait for a taste," he whispered, grinning at her.

She watched horrified as his fangs dropped. When he lowered his head, his lips hovering only a breath from hers, she struck out, her palm glowing red with fire as she struck the side of his head. "*Incendiaire!*"

He bellowed, rolling away and slapping at the flames in his hair. "That was a very bad move, child," he hissed, a burn on his cheek. Charred bits of his long golden hair floated to the ground as he stalked around the bed, eyeing her where she cowered against the headboard.

"Come near me again and I'll burn you to well-done, vampire," she said, forcing bravado into her voice, but knowing she'd do it. She could do it.

He laughed. "Stupid bitch. You cannot even tell that I am like you," he murmured. Lifting one hand, he watched her with a smile.

Shadoe shrieked as an unseen hand closed around her and jerked her up. Something gagged her, keeping her from screaming as she was slammed against a wall and pinned there.

"You will not catch me by surprise again," he said, strolling over to her. "And you're so fucking young, you don't know how to manipulate things without using your mouth or hands, haven't figured out you don't need it. Bad thing about the pathetic Hunters, they insist on muzzling their own, putting blinders on them. By the time you've figured out you don't need to speak…you will not be able to," he said, smiling brightly.

As she whimpered and shrank away from him, he cupped her breast in his hand, circling his thumb over the soft nipple over and over, pinching it until it finally peaked for him.

"Very nice…*oui*. You are a very lovely woman," he murmured. "I'm going to enjoy owning you."

Her eyes blazed at him and he chuckled. "Yes, I know… You think you aren't owned. But you will admit it, by the time I am done. I own you, body, mind…and pussy." He cupped her in his hand and plunged his finger into her dry passage as he spoke, smiling a pleased, satisfied smile. "And what a tight pussy it is."

Fury flooded her and she narrowed her eyes, breathing through her nose as whatever it was threatened to gag her when she tried to drag in enough air to scream. No sound escaped her—but she did feel the ripple of magick. She rarely used words… Benjamin hadn't taught her that way. Her hands, she needed sometimes, or at least she thought she did.

Her eyes opened wide and she let the fury take her.

Wind started to whip.

Heat pooled inside her.

As he jammed his fingers back inside her dry vagina, the heat erupted from her. She didn't seek to control it, just channeled it as it shot from within her to him.

A wall of fire shot up from the floor, a muffled roar that was drowned out by the French bastard's shriek of pain. His hands left her and he was across the room like a shot, cradling his singed arm to his chest. "Little *coquette*. I shall make you hurt for that one," he hissed.

The flames were dying out as he straightened, and Shadoe instinctively flinched. Forming flames, she could do. But she didn't know how to maintain them.

"Little witches who don't know their own powers should really be careful," he murmured.

His eyes closed and Shadoe felt a chill wind brush by her and settle over her. Cold…very cold. It settled into her bones and made her ache deep within. When her eyes opened, she could see, out of the corner of her eye, something dull and gray. But it disappeared when she tried to look at it head on, forever trapped just outside her line of vision.

"That is your cage, *chére*," he purred. "It locks all that magick inside, with you. And it stays inside, with you. If you try to strike out at me, you may not live to regret it…all of your magick is magnified with that sphere. And this could be a very bad thing, especially if you try fire again."

He moved closer, stopping just a few feet away from her face. "This will be...most pleasant," he whispered. "Enjoy your time away from me. I'll be back, once you are ready to control yourself. In the meantime...enjoy your company."

Shadoe nearly choked on bile as Marcus dragged somebody in, a small, slimly built girl, whose frightened eyes wheeled around in their sockets. He threw her at Shadoe's feet, and while she watched, he started to stroke her body as the girl screamed and sobbed.

Shadoe struck out and pain tore through her as the energy bolt of magick reflected back at her, tearing her flesh and burning it.

Marcus laughed as he pried his young woman's thighs apart. "Isn't she sweet? Twenty years old, hot and sweet, and a virgin until twenty minutes ago," he purred as he freed his penis.

Shadoe screamed her fury and lobbed another bolt before she could control it and it launched back at her, this time knocking her out. She fell into the pit of blackness with a sob, the woman's helpless screams chasing her as she went.

* * * * *

Benjamin clung to the shadows as he slid through the woods. Leandra was behind him, her steps nearly as quiet as his.

Malachi was nowhere to be seen, but Benjamin could feel his presence. *Why couldn't he feel her?*

Never before had he cursed his own gift of magick, strong, certain, and sure. But it wasn't strong enough this time. He couldn't feel his woman, couldn't track her magickally, couldn't sense her. He should have been able to think of her face and feel her.

This terrifying blankness would have had him turning into a ravening beast, if not for Leandra's calm assurance.

The witch with the amber eyes was nothing if not good. He suspected her gift damn near rivaled Shadoe's. And she had learned through means other than Excelsior, so her way of using it would be different. And she was a warrior, not a Healer, although he was certain she was a perfectly capable healer.

His lips spread in a cold smile as he came upon a still corpse. Malachi rose out of the darkness, his teeth flashing white, lips unusually dark. "She is there, my friend. And unharmed, for now," he said. Then his face sobered, the smile fading away, his features going cold and still. "There is a Master in there, vampire with magick of his own. He is the one who cast the web of forgetfulness. This pathetic...creature was one of his minions, a werewolf who defected from the pack that is charged with patrolling this area. He is nearing his first century and this vampire was ancient when the wolf came to him."

He stood in the moonlight, absorbing it. "I can feel it...and he knows I am here. A Master cannot physically enter another Master's territory unknown." An evil grin split his face and he said, "I ought to introduce myself." Sliding his eyes to them, he said, "There's the distraction for you—go get your woman, Cross."

His form faded away as he shifted to mist and then even the mist was gone.

Meeting Leandra's eyes, Benjamin asked, "So, how good are you?"

She grinned and reached down, rolling the leg of her black cargo pants up and drawing a wickedly long blade. Benjamin saw the liquid glow of it in the moonlight and surmised it was nearly pure silver. It winked at him as she tossed it from hand to hand. "Keep up if you can, Hunter," she murmured.

And then she took the lead, gliding in and out of the shadows as though she was one with them.

* * * * *

"Wake up, bitch," Marcus purred.

The words whispered out of the darkness, sending black fear streaking through her.

She fought away from it, struggling to cling to the painless oblivion.

Sharp pain rocked her and she whimpered.

It came again, and against her will, she worked her way out of the darkness, opening her eyes just as Marcus drew back his foot, kicking her in the side sharply. The magickally made cage parted around his foot, closing around his leg, keeping her from striking through the hole his strike made.

Her hand flew out and caught his ankle and twisted. She didn't have the energy to smile as he landed on his ass.

Shoving herself up, she settled on her butt with her back to the wall. A horrified moan choked her as she caught sight of the woman lying by the wall, blood staining her thighs, bruises ringing her throat. Shadoe caught the coppery scent of her blood, too much of it. Her breathing was shallow and ragged, wet sounding.

The woman was going to die—by morning, Shadoe's instincts whispered—if she didn't get help.

Marcus lunged to his feet and loomed over her, drawing his leg back, a snarl contorting his face.

"Do it… I'll set loose a firestorm that will burn your leg off at the knee, and damn the consequences," she rasped, the pain in her side stealing her breath.

His response was cut off when the door flew open and the golden-haired vampire came in like a vicious storm, his eyes flashing, face scowling. "There is somebody on my land, somebody ancient, a Master Vampire who isn't touched by any of my spells of protection. He is filled with purpose and drive— my spells rob a person of that. I do not know a single creature that can withstand my magick. But I have heard tales of a vampire who just might be able."

Though the bastard never once mentioned a name, Shadoe knew damn well who it was—Malachi. Unconsciously, a tiny smile curved her lips.

The rage rolling from him would have made her quiver with fear, except she could sense the fear that was fueling that powerful rage. Fear of Malachi, she suspected.

"I thought you said she belonged to an Inherent," Dumas growled.

He stared at Shadoe with rage in his eyes before moving his furious gaze to Marcus. "If you have led Hunters to my door, and if he is one of them, I will have your hide, cured and tanned, on my wall for all to see," he promised softly.

"Pierre, the bitch was fucking some bastard wolf. There was a vampire, but if he is so powerful, he would have enthralled her and she'd never go running back to that bastard, Cross."

Shadoe couldn't stop the smile that spread across her face anymore than she could muffle her snort of laughter.

Pierre…what a name, she thought with laughter. He tossed her a venomous look and responded, "I do not think she agrees with you." He moved toward her, with a loose, liquid walk, his body a seductive promise as he knelt beside her. "Who is this vampire who was so lucky to have a taste of that sweet pussy?" he asked silkily.

She stared at him in stony silence.

He swore softly, reaching through the unseen barrier and cupping her face in his hand. "I can make you tell me, bitch. Do you want… What is this?" he asked, frowning, brushing her hair aside and revealing the faintest of marks of her neck.

The bite had nearly healed completely. It wouldn't even leave a scar. But it was still visible, if you looked.

And he was looking. Brushing his hand against it, everything went still as his rage grew almost palpable. "You've brought me used goods. I do not want another vampire's leavings," Pierre whispered, his voice an insidious hiss that made Shadoe think of snakes, slithering and writhing together. Every word sent fear coursing through her, and the fear grew, overtaking her mind.

Not real... He's making me feel this way...not real. Not real...
Clenching her eyes closed, she focused, trying to think past the
fear. Miraculously, it fell away and she sucked in a ragged
breath, wincing as her ribs protested. Opening her eyes, she
stared at Pierre who narrowed his eyes at what he saw in her
face.

"A strong, powerful thing you'll be...if I let you live,"
Pierre whispered. "And it will be greatly in your favor if you tell
me what I want to know. Tell me of this vampire."

Her eyes never wavered and she didn't say a word.

Rising, he turned, his bare chest rippling as he took a slow,
deep breath. She suspected he was trying to calm the great rage
she sensed within him. Great rage...and fear.

He feared the Hunters. He must, otherwise he wouldn't live
as he did, in shadows, erasing all signs of himself before the
Hunters could track him.

"Tell me of this vampire you saw her with," Pierre
murmured, stalking around Marcus in a close circle. Stopping
behind him, he murmured right into Marcus' ear, his voice silky,
seductive. "Tell me..."

Shadoe could feel the hot, mind-fogging lust that he
exuded. Using it to control Marcus, she realized. And it was
working. She saw the unwitting arousal bloom in his face,
watched as his cock started to tent his trousers. "Big, pale, red-
haired. I heard her call his name... *Malcolm...Malachi...*yes,
Malachi."

Shadoe shivered as Pierre lifted his gaze, and she saw the
fear and rage explode in his eyes, watched the deadly smile that
curved his mouth. Marcus, however, with his back to the
vampire was unaware of anything except the hot, lustful waves
that rolled through the room.

She was unaffected, whether by her fear or by her own
magick, she didn't know. She watched with undisguised horror
as Pierre stroked Marcus' short, curly brown locks, fisting his
hand. Marcus shuddered as though in ecstasy. Now another

scent filled the air, that of the shape-shifter's hunger, a scent she was familiar with. He was horny.

He opened eyes dazed by need and licked his lips, unaware of the death that stood at his back.

And Shadoe flinched as Pierre struck, sinking his fangs into the line of Marcus' neck as he jerked the Inherent's head to the side, arching and baring it.

Marcus moaned, like a man caught in the throes of ecstasy.

He was moaning until he passed out from blood loss, nearly fifteen minutes later. A wet stain had bloomed on his trousers and she smelled the unmistakable scent of semen The vampire had brought him to orgasm as he fed. Jerking his head sharply, Pierre drew back, licking his lips. She was surprised to see his tongue wasn't forked. The hideous sound of flesh tearing was one she would never forget. A huge, hideous hole appeared in Marcus' neck and blood pumped from it in a steady flow.

Dropping the limp body to the floor, he turned his gaze her way, and Shadoe shivered at the burning light of his green eyes. "I'll be back for you later, little Hunter bitch," Pierre swore. "I have not fought this long to fall at the hands of your lover. I do not care that he is the fabled Malachi. He is outnumbered, outclassed... He will die for daring to come to my lands."

She didn't dare argue with him. If she told him Benjamin was her lover, he may realize that he had more than Malachi to deal with.

But the factor of surprise could work in their favor. No, she told herself. It *would* work in their favor. It had to.

She was left alone in the room as Marcus bled to death through the gaping hole Pierre had torn in his throat before dropping him.

* * * * *

Malachi simply alighted on the grand porch and waited, flinging his large frame onto the padded chaise lounge, staring up at the sky, listening to the baying of the wolves who were trying to track him.

Of course, they were searching the wrong area.

I'm up here, he thought, unable to stop the grin that curved his mouth.

And they weren't searching Benjamin's area either. The wolf was pulling the Inherent deal, menace rolling from him in silent waves. Lesser wolves would instinctively avoid the area around Benjamin, not even aware of why. When the door blew open and the vampire stepped through, Malachi continued to lie there, fighting back the urge to start whistling under his breath.

"Find him, damn it," the vampire rasped. The power of his voice alone would have been enough to make some people pause.

Malachi grinned.

More wolves swarmed out of the house, some wolven, some in wolfman form, beyond them, vampires flowed out in silent waves.

Nearly twenty people, and all searching for a man who was waiting right there. *Not much on searching for brains amongst your followers, are you?* Malachi mused. Granted, he was not dead in their line of sight, a good twenty feet to the side, and the veranda was dark.

He might not be breathing, and they couldn't hear a heartbeat that sounded only infrequently.

But Hell, they could have *smelled* him.

These weren't mortals, who didn't always think to look beyond what they could see in front of them. A paranormal should remember that, and Malachi knew damn well a legion of Hunters could have passed by him, and every damn one of them would have *looked* for him.

None of them would have been that stupid.

Because if they were, Malachi was who they would deal with when lives were lost.

With a lazy stretch, Malachi moved and drew attention to himself. "Such an intelligent bunch you have there," he said, laughter thick in his voice.

The eyes that flew to his face were wide with astonishment, then malice filtered through. "It truly is the esteemed Malachi, feared by all, the most powerful and ancient of the Hunters," Pierre murmured, a wide grin curving his mouth. "I never thought the day would come when I'd draw the attention of the mighty one himself. I always assumed you'd send your underlings to deal with me, if ever I was discovered.

"Although," he mused, tapping a finger to his chin. "I imagine my taking your lover had something to do with it."

He paused and lifted his hand to his nose, breathing in deep.

Malachi's lip curled and he had to remind himself to blank his face. He knew what the bastard was up to—Mal could scent the musk of Shadoe's body, faint as it was. Benjamin would kill him, assuming Malachi left anything behind.

"She smells so sweet… I can hardly wait to taste."

Malachi didn't respond to that as he moved closer. "I do not like killing men until I know their names. What is yours?"

Apparently he didn't like Mal's lack of response to his taunt. "Pierre Dumas. Your bitch will scream my name before the night is over," he snarled, flashing his fangs and flinging a hand at Malachi.

Mal moved away from the fire, shifting to mist as the second blast came winging at him. "Pete, you should really get some new hooks when you try to piss somebody off. The threat to rape my woman, probably over my dead body, is one that has been used more times than I can count," Malachi said, settling back to human form a few feet behind Pierre. He didn't bother addressing the little mistake about Shadoe not being his woman. Might as well give Benjamin all the advantage he could.

"But why waste it? Particularly when it's so very true," Pierre swore. "I'll put my hands on her, though, and when she has no shields between us, she will fall under my thrall and scream for completion as I rip your head away from your body. She'll scream for me, for me to love her, to fuck, to rape her, to hurt her, whatever I desire. I'll fuck her in a puddle of your blood."

Malachi sidestepped the blow, moving quicker than human eyes could track. "You have to spill enough of it first," he said calmly. "So far, you canna even manage to lay a bloody hand on me."

"I will not have to—I can always settle for fucking her in your ashes," Pierre rasped as he drew his hand back and flung it forward, as though throwing a baseball, only what came flying forward was a ball of fire.

Bloody hell, really a witch... Malachi barely had time to decide that he would actually have his hands full before he had to flip out of the way. *A witch and a vampire, how the bloody hell?*

* * * * *

Leandra laid her hand on the house.

Benjamin could feel the shield she was boring through, but only just now. If she hadn't laid her hands on it, Benjamin wasn't sure if he would have seen it in time. "Da witch dat laid this spun it out of himself. If we break it, it will weaken him. If he's da vampire that Malachi was sensing, dis will lay him low for a few moments. How long, I don't know."

"Malachi doesn't need our help," Benjamin muttered, distracted. He was feeling...*something*...

"He stripped Shadoe of her shields," Leandra muttered. "Once we get through these, you will feel her again." She looked like a cat burglar, working some unseen lock, as Benjamin focused his gaze on her hands.

"I can already feel something," he whispered, his big body shuddering, vibrating. He could feel the animal inside him trying to tear free. A soft, familiar voice whispered... *Patience.* The Wolf's image shimmered into view just behind Ben's eyes, so that he had to focus to actually see what was in front of him, instead of the Wolf.

Patience...listen to your head, right now, not your heart. Act like a Hunter.

"I am a Hunter. I think I can manage," Benjamin growled. Then the shield underneath Leandra's hands fell apart.

And all he could feel was Shadoe's terror and horror, and he tore through the widening hole, his body shifting from human to wolfman in three lunges. Leandra, still frozen as she worked in demolishing the whole of the shield, swore softly. "Damn it, Cross, use your damn head!"

But Benjamin was already tearing down the hall, following the direction of his heart.

Shadoe screamed as the door flew open.

When the wolf tore through, she buried her face in her hands, whimpering. Damn it, no more...no more! Screaming it, her hands stiffened and went to her sides, clenched into tight fists. "No more!"

And then she sobbed, "Ben!"

He went from wolfman to his mortal skin as he stepped to her, the change liquid and seamless. Laying his hands on the shield, he whispered, "Be quiet...don't move, don't breathe... I'll get you out of this."

The shield was easily broken from without, and a few seconds later, she collapsed against Benjamin. Throwing her arms around his neck and sobbing, she buried her face against his chest.

"It's all right, sweet, all right, shhh," he murmured, shielding her from seeing the pooling blood and the cooling body with his own, now naked form. His clothes were lying wherever he had shifted, she knew, and she reveled in the heat of his body. She was so cold...so damned cold.

"Damn it, Shadoe...look at me," she heard him shout, but it was a distant sound.

"You're going into shock—listen to me, listen!" he demanded and his voice was so insistent, she looked at him...and listened.

Listened to his voice as he rubbed his hands up and down her arms, watched his lips moving as he spoke.

* * * * *

Leandra paused outside the door, checking on Ben and Shadoe. She looked shocky, but Benjamin was taking care of her. Leandra had to take care of them. This house was too big, too open. Too many places for evil to hide and lurk.

She ought to know, after all, she hadn't spent her formative years in charm school.

As she walked, she whispered a spell of her making. A web sort of spell, with her as the center and only those she allowed in or out would be able to approach the house. Any vampire, mortal or shifter caught within her web without her consent would die. The web was the house, and the more of it she saw, the larger the web grew.

A soft, muffled curse reached her ears, one that was in a soft, Scottish burr. The snarling and growling that came to her made her belly roll and pitch with fear. The vampire wasn't playing nice anymore. He had called for reinforcements, in the shape of hellhounds. She broke into a run as she swore, following the sound of the baying, and the stink of the evil magick.

Somehow the vampire had managed to leash a small hellpower, and he cast it like he knew how to use it. The hounds appeared just as Leandra tumbled to a stop at the door of the house. Her web had worked, keeping all she didn't allow out and the hounds that struck the invisible line of the web fell away baying in pain.

But they had Malachi cornered, and he was bleeding. Badly.

Not even Malachi could fight that many of the hounds.

And the vampire watching knew it.

Blood trickled from his mouth as he pushed up, but there was evil pleasure in his eyes as he watched another hound launch itself at Malachi and land on his back. This one was a small one, roughly the size of an Irish wolfhound, but when he opened his mouth, Leandra froze. His teeth were yellow and dripping. The fluid seeped through Malachi's shirt and he bellowed, swearing.

"Poison," she whispered soundlessly.

She swallowed and the sound was a dry click in her throat. Taking a deep breath, she stepped through the web, changing the nature of the spell as she moved, and letting it center on Benjamin and Shadoe. Brushing against Shadoe's mind, she assured herself the witch would be fine.

Leandra, suddenly, wasn't so certain about herself.

Malachi could fight off the hound's poison, but not if he kept getting struck, and not if he didn't get away soon. They needed another target.

A rogue witch who was also vampire, such a foul creature should never have survived his creation.

"C'mon, puppies…" Leandra started, her voice singsong, not revealing any of the terrible fear she felt.

Malachi's eyes widened and he swore. "Get back, damn it!"

The vampire on the floor was pushing himself to his knees, bleeding from a myriad of injuries, his mouth swollen and cut, but knitting together, smoothing out even as she watched.

"Jacob!" the vampire bellowed.

"If ya call for your wolves…well, you'll have to expend some energy to get them here. Dey are…rather lost," she said. "In a maze I made for dem before we busted through your pathetic shields."

Turning her eyes to the hounds, she released what was sure to attract them—fiery, shining displays of magick. "Make sure Benjamin gets Shadoe out of here," she said, her voice calm.

But on the inside, she was screaming.

Now that it had come down to it, Leandra had decided, she really didn't want to die.

But it took a witch to fight hellhounds, to destroy them. Just as it took a witch to call them.

They leaped, and as they struck her shielding, the baying started.

* * * * *

Malachi couldn't cross whatever barrier she had set up.

Dropping his own shielding, he bellowed, "*Cross!*" The paralyzing fear he was capable of exploded from him, and the weaker hounds fell prey to it, as did many of the witch-vampire's minions. The howls of pain and fear started. Malachi heard the roar of shrieking and sobbing out beyond the veranda and suspected Leandra's little maze was built on an illusion that hid them from sight as well.

Benjamin appeared at his side, Shadoe cradled in his arms, her eyes wide and far too dark.

"Get her out of here," Malachi ordered, his eyes on the witch he could barely see beneath the hides of the hounds. So many...too many. Not even a witch as powerful as Leandra could fight that many alone. Not when Dumas was pushing to his feet, eyeing Leandra with hatred and rage.

And hunger...Malachi went rigid as he saw the calculation in that gaze. Yes, a witch like Leandra would make a tasty meal. But more...Leandra *was* still human, like Shadoe was not. He could almost see the wheel's spinning in Dumas' mind.

Malachi could see Dumas' lips moving as he called more hounds.

"Shit, she can't fight that many hounds," Cross swore. "And she damn well knows it."

"I told you to leave," Malachi said, his fangs dropped in his fury. Lifting his hands, he laid them on the still unseen shield. It burned into his flesh and he swore, clenching his teeth against the pain. With a whisper of power, he shifted to mist and flowed over the shield, searching for the entry, a weak point where he could slide in.

"Screw that," Benjamin swore, kneeling and laying Shadoe against the wall. Her eyes flew to his, and Malachi could sense the rabid fear that filled her. "Sweet, Leandra needs me...shhh, just wait here."

Shadoe's eyes closed and Mal sensed the battle she waged against her fear. When her eyes opened, clear and focused, he saw she had won that battle. "Go," she said hoarsely. "I'll be fine." Bracing her back against the wall, she prepared to wait.

Malachi grimaced as he felt Benjamin's magick strike the shield. But it was too damn strong, and they both knew it.

Malachi shifted back to mortal form, swearing.

"I can break through," Shadoe said softly, still sitting on the ground, clutching her knees to her chest. Her eyes were glowing, the unseen winds of witch power blowing her hair all around her.

They could feel it, a needle's lance of power, striking the shield and boring through. "Careful how you go, pet," Malachi whispered, watching Leandra. "Don't go damaging the maker."

Benjamin's face was pale and he said, "I'm taking care of that... Shadoe's magick is still too raw. Get ready...it's about to break."

When it did, it was with a dull roar of power and Malachi flipped into the air as hounds launched themselves free of the dying shield. He rasped out a muttered, "*Fuck*," and shot Shadoe a desperate look. Her magick would call to them, just like Leandra's had.

But Shadoe was sitting untouched in a small semi-circle of clear space, the hounds snarling and gnashing at her from feet away, unable to reach her. "Smart girl," Malachi murmured.

A pain-filled shriek rent the air and Malachi launched himself at the source. "Leandra, on the other hand, is a foolish one," he muttered to himself. A hound's claws raked his arm as he tried to power through their writhing masses. Unsuccessful with strength, he shifted to mist and reformed at her side as she slapped out with a glowing hand to beat at the hound that had sunk his teeth into her thigh.

She was bleeding from a dozen different wounds.

Something large and furred leaped into the small circle and Malachi turned, fangs bared and hand fisted, only to see Benjamin sinking one huge, deadly hand, tipped with ebony claws, into the side of the nearest hound. Smoke emanated from the hound's mouth as it howled, and then the light died from its eyes as Benjamin crushed and burned his heart.

Another wave of hounds struck, and the three of them battled them back, the witches with fire, Malachi with strength.

"Somebody has to face the vampire," Benjamin grunted, closing his eyes for a brief second. When they opened, flame surrounded them, trapping most of the hounds behind it, blocking them. Malachi caught the one that lunged at him and ripped it apart, severing the head from the long serpentine body and flinging the pieces into the fire.

"It can't be me," Benjamin panted, catching Malachi's arm before he could attack another of the hounds. Staring into the ancient one's face, he repeated harshly, "It can't be me. I may be a powerful witch, but he's better. You're not a witch, but you can handle witchcraft in ways no vampire should be able to do. He's hidden from us for this long—we can't allow him to keep hiding. He has to die. And that means *you* have to face him."

Benjamin waited, holding his breath, until Mal nodded. Then Ben turned and faced the hounds, calling upon ice as he placed himself at Leandra's back. When he looked again, Malachi was gone.

"Get out of here," Leandra snapped. "Are ya stupid?"

"I love you, too," he said with a slight smile as he concentrated on the spell building in his hands. They ached with the cold. Eying the hounds, he waited until the closest two lunged and then he unleashed it. They were hit with a rain of ice, freezing the first line of hounds solid, and several of the others behind them disappeared in a puff of smoke, fleeing the deadly cold.

When he had time to focus on their numbers again, he decided there were fewer of them.

"Dere's not as many. Malachi must be distracting him," Leandra panted.

"Good." Benjamin forged a shield between them and the hounds, a writhing ring of smoke that shifted and danced, reforming each time a hound tried to break through. "That will keep them busy for a while. Let's see to your leg."

He had just finished leeching the poison out of the nasty bite when they heard Shadoe scream.

Shadoe's breath locked in her lungs. He wasn't real. Couldn't be real…*couldn't be real*.

Jimmy was *dead*.

Malachi slammed Dumas to the ground, lifting his head, preparing to strike. Shadoe's scream made him pause.

Dumas laughed.

"You had better hurry, *mon ami*," the battered vampire said, blood pouring from his lips. "She sounds very frightened."

Malachi drew a silver knife from his thigh and waggled it tauntingly. "Since I can't take the time to bleed you…let me give ye a parting gift," he purred. Driving the deadly blade into Dumas' heart, he twisted it, listening to the vampire scream as smoke poured from him.

As battered as he was, he wasn't able to throw Malachi off and Dumas just lay there, screaming that hideous shriek as Malachi darted away, following the sounds of Shadoe's sobs.

"Go," Leandra ordered, bracing her back against one of the pillars of the veranda-styled porch. Her face was pale and beaded with sweat, her eyes glassy with pain and blood loss. Her leg was slick with her own blood, necessary for letting the poison out. But damned weakening. "I'll be fine."

Benjamin hesitated for the briefest of seconds before he tore through the ring of smoke still protecting them. When he got to Shadoe, he saw her screaming at a slim, wraith-like woman. Then he blinked and saw a man he had only seen in newspaper clippings. Jimmy Duncan. Another blink, and the woman…*illusion*. A bloody witch.

She was terrifying Shadoe with the one thing that was guaranteed to horrify her into helplessness. With a roar, he grabbed the woman before she even realized he was on her and snapped her neck. For some odd reason, witches rarely expected a physical attack.

Malachi appeared out of the melee as Benjamin let her fall dead to the ground.

"Illusion, she was making Shadoe think she was somebody else. Damn witch was playing with her mind," Benjamin murmured, laying a hand on the shield Shadoe had up. "Baby, it's okay. He's not really here. Let me in."

Shadoe's shields collapsed, Ben knelt and took her in his arms. But he had barely nestled her against him when a tremendous mental explosion shook him as the smoke-shield he had left around Leandra shattered.

There was silence.

The night was filled with drifting bits of fire, wild magick and smoke, frightened hounds darting here and there, launching themselves at any target and fleeing at any movement. Their summoner had lost purpose or was focused elsewhere, so the hounds were easily distracted and easily scared away now.

Benjamin didn't like what that could mean.

If the vampire that had summoned them was dead, the hounds would have fled, running to seek havoc wherever they could. That they were still here, running aimlessly, didn't bode well.

Taking Shadoe in his arms, he pushed to his feet, weak and shaky. Malachi scowled as he took that in. "What the bloody hell?" he demanded, bracing him with a hand under his arm.

"My shields were shattered," Benjamin said shortly. "Leandra was inside them." His eyes were grim, and he forced himself not to think—not yet.

He started forward, silently accepting the support from Malachi as they returned to where Benjamin had left Leandra.

Dumas looked up from where he was feeding at Leandra's neck, his eyes glowing, an unholy smile on his lips as he pulled away, letting her fall limp to the floor. "Thank you, *mon ami*, for removing that nasty poison from her blood. A powerful, plentiful meal, and I feel…refreshed. Too bad I had to damn near drain what little blood you left from purging her," he said with laughter.

Before Malachi could attack, he shifted to mist and was gone. They were left alone with Leandra's still body, impotent fear and rage filling all of them.

Sinking to his knees, Malachi took her in his arms, pressing his thumb against the seeping wound and sealing it. "She's almost gone," he said bleakly, his eyes stark and desolate.

"Bring her over," Benjamin snarled. As he laid Shadoe down, her haunted blue eyes moved to Leandra's body. Slowly, painfully, she rolled over, laying a hand on Leandra's still chest. Benjamin knelt by her head, stroking those long, heavy rows of braids, his eyes full of rage, guilt and grief. "Bring her over, damn it. Now."

Malachi shook his head. "No. You think she would want that? Walking in darkness for always?"

"She doesn't want death," Shadoe whispered, lifting tear-drenched eyes to Malachi's. "I can feel her. She actually wants to live, for the first time in years. Don't let her die, Mal. Please."

The ancient one's eyes closed and he cupped Leandra's face in his hands, shaking his head. "She can't possibly want this." But she didn't want to die, he could feel that. She didn't understand what was happening, what was going on outside her body, but she did know she was dying.

And she was terrified and furious.

"She's a witch… She'll not be trapped the way many vampires are," Benjamin argued.

"And the change could damn well kill her," Malachi snapped even as he absorbed some of the desperation coming from the dying witch. Her heart was starting to falter, her breathing becoming erratic. Whatever they were going to do, time was running short.

Benjamin's laughter was a harsh bark in the silence. "She's going to *die* regardless. At least if you bring her over, she has a chance. Now, *do* it. Otherwise, I'm gonna come after your ass."

"She very well might hate us all for this," Malachi said coldly, ignoring Ben.

Shadoe's eyes opened, tears spilling over to run down her pale face. "No, she won't. Hurry, Mal. I can't feel her anymore."

Even though her blood was potent and sweet, Malachi had never regretted a feeding more. Drawing from the still witch was bitter, and he damned himself. Once he had taken what he needed for the bond, he tore a vein open in his wrist and held it to her ashen mouth, stroking her throat to force his blood down.

He felt her soul hurtling back into her body, although her eyes didn't open immediately.

They wouldn't.

Not until nightfall next.

Chapter Thirteen

Shadoe slept, Leandra in the bed next to her.

Malachi and Benjamin had gone back to burn the plantation to the ground. The anonymous hotel room was the safest they would get for now. But Malachi would be going after the vampire who had nearly destroyed them all. She had seen it in his eyes.

As she slept, and dreamed, part of her worried.

Shadoe woke for a few brief moments, just before nightfall, but the exhaustion pulled at her and when she saw that Leandra still slept — still *lived* — she closed her eyes and slid back into the arms of sleep.

Leandra had slept all through the first night.

Malachi had said she would wake tonight, if she was going to.

Shadoe woke again before sunrise and showered quickly, sliding back into the shirt one of the men had put her in before she went back to sit on the bed and watch the still woman as she slept. Her chest rose infrequently. Shadoe's sharp hearing occasionally picked up a heartbeat.

What kind of creature would she be?

Had they done the wrong thing?

Could the change push her into madness?

Shadoe didn't know enough about vampires...but Benjamin would. If it was likely to turn her mad, he wouldn't have insisted Malachi do it. And Malachi wouldn't have done it, no matter what anybody said if it was going to unleash a monster on the earth.

And Leandra wouldn't have wanted that.

A thousand worries chased themselves over in Shadoe's mind and she finally leapt up off the bed, pacing. When the door opened, she screamed, so caught up in her worrying, she hadn't even heard them coming. Thankfully, it was Ben and Mal staring at her with bemusement, and not werewolves that Dumas had sent after her.

Flinging herself at Benjamin, she whispered, "What if we've done the wrong thing?"

He stroked his hand down her hair, murmuring, "It will be okay. I promise."

"Too late to worry now… She's coming back," Malachi said obliquely.

How he knew that, Shadoe didn't know. Staring at Leandra's face, she saw nothing, felt nothing. And nearly an hour passed before anything changed. When her eyes opened, Shadoe was sitting on the bed, stroking the coarse braids absently, not seeing anything but the sight of the vampire as he dropped Leandra to the ground, his mouth stained with her blood.

"You're safe," Leandra said, her voice husky. She smiled, a sweet, happy curve of her full, wide mouth that made Shadoe's eyes sting.

"Yes, I am. Thank you for helping them." She licked her lips, unsure what to say. Leandra's eyes studied her face, moved to Benjamin's, then to Malachi's.

She was far too calm. Malachi had said she would most likely awaken frightened, screaming, and that they needed to be prepared to slam shields down on her.

But she was…calm.

"Something is wrong, isn't it?" Leandra asked quietly, a frown marring her exotic features. Her eyes clouded and Shadoe could see her thinking. *She doesn't remember…* "What happened?"

She swallowed then, and winced. The bite from Malachi had faded, healed thanks to her wondrous new vampire metabolism. But the larger, nasty jagged bite from Dumas remained, smaller, healing, but not gone. Her hand came up to touch it, and Shadoe watched with tears in her eyes as Leandra probed it and started to recall. "De vampire... He came up and broke Ben's shield. I didn't even see him, not until it was too late. He grabbed me, froze me with a mind spell...and he bit me."

Her eyes closed and her mouth spasmed. Shadoe reached out and folded her hand around one of Leandra's, the hot tears burning her face. "He bit me, whispering into m' mind..." Leandra whispered, clutching desperately at Shadoe's hand. "Why aren't I dead?"

"Malachi..."

Before Benjamin could finish his sentence, Malachi stepped up, his face grim. "I brought you over. I knew the consequences, regardless of the arguments Shadoe and Benjamin may give in my favor, I knew them. If anybody is deserving of your anger, your hatred, it is me, not them," he said quietly, dropping to one knee by the bed, meeting her eyes levelly.

"Brought me over," she repeated.

Malachi inclined his head.

Silence reigned.

Slowly, Leandra sat up, tugging her hand gently away from Shadoe's. "I remember tinking," she said quietly, "as I went to face de hounds dat I really wasn't ready to die."

She licked her lips. Her fangs hadn't yet broken through, although she knew they would, sometime that night. Her eyes closed, and she gave a brief moment's mourning to the sunrises she'd never see. But she was *alive*. And that was exactly how she wanted to be.

"I didn't want to be dead. I *don't* want to be dead," she said vehemently.

Rising, she whispered, "I need to tink."

Her legs quivered and shook as she walked outside.

Once outside in the moonlight, she collapsed.

* * * * *

Malachi swore roughly. "She's not dead, damn it."

"She knows that," Shadoe said quietly, leaning over the bed and kissing him lightly. "She needs to think. Like she said."

He smiled tightly. "The lady has not had the easiest of lives. She deserves something easy…not this."

"Nothing in life is ever easy, especially not for a Hunter," Benjamin said softly, resting a hand on Mal's shoulder. "It will be okay. She will be okay."

"I hope so," Malachi murmured. Rising, he took Shadoe's hand and bowed over it, lifting it to his lips. "Milady. Such a wise, wonderful witch you've become, and so fast."

Then he shifted to mist, the echo of his voice floating through the room. "I'm going Hunting…for now."

Benjamin couldn't have gotten Malachi and Leandra out of the room any quicker if he had wished it.

As the echo of Mal's voice faded from the room, he approached the bed, reaching down and pulling Shadoe to her feet, slanting his mouth roughly across hers. Her arms, slender and strong, wound desperately around his neck, holding him to her tightly as he tore at her clothes.

Pulling his mouth away, he glared down at her and swore, "If you ever leave me again, *for anything*, I'm going to tan your hide. No, I'll pink it. I'll spank you so damn hard, you'll feel my hand on your ass for a month." His heart swelled painfully in his chest and he rested his brow on hers. "Damn it, baby. Don't ever do that again… I love you so much. I was so fucking scared I'd never see you again, that he'd hurt you…"

"I love you," she whispered into his mouth. "I'm sorry. Spank me, I deserve it."

He laughed. "No. I think you'd like it. You don't get a reward for scaring me to death," he said with a mock scowl.

Then he cupped her face in his hands. "I love you…Shadoe Wallace…Jillian Morgan…both of you, all of you."

She gave a watery laugh. "That's a good thing. Jillian is the one who freaked at the vampire's. Shadoe's a little bit stronger."

He smiled, pressing a gentle kiss to her mouth. "You're both incredibly strong. They are both you. And you are amazing, and *mine*."

"I'm sorry I went with Marcus. I shouldn't have… You could have done something. I know that now," she said, swallowing, licking her lips and looking away. "I'm not used to having anybody to depend on."

"We'll take care of that," he murmured, sliding his hands under her shirt. "I'm going to change it so that I'm the first thing you think of with everything that comes…and speaking of coming…" He grinned wickedly and sank to his knees, pressing his mouth to the vee of her thighs. Spreading her thighs, he lifted one and propped it on his shoulder, opening her, before he pushed his tongue inside her with slow, sensuous movements, nuzzling her clit with his nose, fucking her tight pussy with thorough strokes of his tongue until she was rocking against his mouth and clutching at the back of his head.

He tumbled her back against the bed and shoved her thighs wide, using his thumbs to part her sex, staring at the reddened folds of her pussy for a long moment before lowering his head and drawing his tongue up the cream-drenched slit. "Yummy," he purred, smiling as the vibrations of his voice had her shaking.

"Ben," she sobbed, clutching his head and pushing her cleft against his face eagerly.

He muttered, "Be still. Think of this as your punishment for scaring me to death." Then he set about driving her thoroughly insane as he slowly ate her out, sucking her clit for long moments, finger-fucking her until she was begging to come, backing off just before she hit climax.

Then Ben started to plunge his tongue inside her weeping pussy while he speared the tender hole of her ass with one long, agile index finger. She shrieked and rocked up to meet each diabolical thrust of his tongue, her hands knotted in his hair. He grunted when she pulled, the sharp pain distracting him just slightly from the sweet pleasure of her cream on his tongue, and the hot silk of her ass clenching around his invading finger.

"I'm gonna fuck you until you scream," he growled. "And then I'm gonna flip you over and fuck your ass until you beg for mercy."

"I'm begging now—let me come," she demanded, arching her hips higher and rocking against him, trying to get the angle she needed for climax.

"Not yet...not yet," he purred. Pulling back, he settled on his heels and slowly pulled his shirt off, smiling as her eyes landed on the flexing muscles of his belly and chest, lingering on the bulging biceps as he threw the shirt aside.

Her eyes again dropped to his belly and Benjamin felt his cock jerk in response even as he started to tug at the buttons of his fly. "I want to feel your mouth on me first," he said gruffly, freeing his cock and standing, shoving his jeans off and kicking them away. He pulled her off the bed and shoved her to her knees, wrapping his hand in the tumbled silk of her brunette curls. "Like this... I want to see you on your knees, and my cock in your mouth."

Heat flared in her eyes and she reached up, wrapping one hand around the base of his cock, feeling the pulse of the blood just below the skin, feeling the silk-wrapped steel of his erection. Her belly clenched as she drew her hand up and down his length in one long, slow motion.

Leaning forward, Shadoe licked a wet trail up the throbbing vein on the underside of his length. "In your mouth," he grunted, rocking his hips forward. "Take me in your mouth."

A tiny smile curved her lips as she dipped her head and lapped at his balls instead, raking the sensitive flesh with her teeth.

He snarled and gripped her head between his hands, putting pressure on her jaw until her mouth opened with a surprised "Oh". Then he pushed the aching head of his shaft inside with a growl. "I said, take me in your mouth, damn it. Suck on me."

Shadoe felt his words in the very depths of her core, cream flooding her. Her skin felt five sizes too small and hot, *achy*. Her nipples drew tight, her clit throbbed and she was so damned turned on, one touch on her swollen clit and she knew she'd come. Sliding her mouth up and down in a shallow caress on his cock, she continued her teasing, even with his warning grip on her head.

She was playing with fire and damn it, she loved it.

Especially after the gut-wrenching fear, thinking she'd never see him again.

With one hand, she cupped his sac, stroking the heavy weight of his balls as she licked another slow, teasing trail up and down his length before taking the head of his cock back into her mouth.

His sex jerked and throbbed in her mouth, thick and hard, salty and warm. A drop of fluid seeped out and she sucked it down eagerly, swirling her tongue across the head before resuming her slow, shallow caresses.

"Deeper," he ordered, and then he just pushed deeper, holding her head still and starting to fuck her mouth, as though tired of her teasing.

Staring up through her lashes at him, she shivered as she saw the dark, hungry look in his eyes. For a moment, Shadoe resisted as much as she could, just to tease him, using the considerable strength in her neck and mouth to pull back, to bite down gently until he was swearing.

"Damn it, suck me, Shadoe," he barked. "Take me in deeper." His voice was ragged and his body trembling.

In response…she bit him. Gently, but still, she bit him.

He roared and jerked her to her feet, throwing her to her back and sprawling across her, yanking her hands over her head and holding them in one of his. With his other hand, he spanked her pussy and growled, "You like to play with fire?"

She came, in one quick hard burst that soaked her thighs, and racked her belly with tremors. When she could breathe again, she grinned up at him and said, "I like to play with you...does that count?"

He froze, and then a grin cracked his face. "Tease." Lowering his head, he nibbled her lips gently, kissing her sweetly, all desperation and roughness just suddenly gone. "I love you so much... Are you going to marry me and put me out of my misery?"

A grin so brilliant, it damn near eclipsed the stars outside in brightness, lit her face. Tugging her hands, she waited until he let her go and then she threw them around his neck and murmured, "Damn straight I'll marry you. Just as soon as you make love to me."

"Hmmm...with pleasure," he whispered, hooking his arms under hers so he could cup her head in his hands, slanting his mouth over hers and pushing his tongue into her mouth. He probed between her thighs and slid easily into her wet core, groaning into her mouth as she closed around him like a hungry, silky fist.

Pumping his hips slowly, he made love to her, feeling her heart pounding against his, her tongue tangling with his. The walls of her pussy hugged his cock tightly and her nipples stabbed into his chest, sharp, hot little diamonds of sensation.

The hot walls of her sheath clenched and tightened around him, milking his cock as he stroked deep inside her. A flush spread from her breasts up to her neck, pinkening her cheeks as she watched him through slitted eyes.

"You're so damned pretty," he muttered against her lips, shifting his grip on her hands so that their fingers were laced palm to palm.

Each time she started to near climax, he backed off, shifting his angle, changing his pace. "Not yet," he whispered when she sobbed out her frustration. "Not yet...just feel it. Do you feel me inside you? Damn it, I can feel you, so tight, so hot. You're mine — all mine."

"And you're mine," she gasped, as he moved higher on her body, dragging his body teasingly against her clit. Her clit ached and throbbed, the need for climax riding her so hard, she could barely breathe with it. "Damn it, Ben...let me come!"

"No," he whispered against her ear with a grin. "I told you I was going to fuck you until you screamed."

Her lashes lifted as she stared at him, her body shivering all over with the need to come. He stared right back at her, a teasing light in his eyes, as he lowered his head to her ear and whispered, "You have to scream..."

She did scream, then, with sheer frustration, arching her hips and hooking her legs around his waist, tightening her pussy around him in a slow, sensuous caress, narrowing her eyes to slits as she stared up at him, her hair damp and tangled around her shoulders.

A look of tortured bliss crossed his face and she bore down on him again, squeezing his cock with her inner muscles, flashing him a slow, sultry smile.

He groaned and slammed into her, lowering his head and sinking his teeth into her shoulder, hard enough to leave a mark, to brand. He pulled out, driving into her again with bruising force, over and over, until she shrieked, the climax storming out of her and racking her entire body with shudders, her pussy clamping forcefully on his plunging cock.

"Baby," he grunted. "So fucking tight..." He sank back in and held still as he started to come, his cock jerking as his seed spilled into her, hot thick streams that flooded her womb as she floated down from her orgasm.

Still hard, he pulled out of her, and flipped her over onto her belly, staring at her exposed rump with a smile. Stroking his finger down the crevice of her ass, he purred, "Get ready for this."

The bed squeaked as he moved away. Shadoe couldn't even breathe, much less move. When he returned, she wheezed out a tortured, "You're insane…" as he started to coat her anus with something cool and slick.

"No. Just dying for you," he said softly, pushing a long, slick finger inside, probing, wiggling. Then he added a second. She sobbed, heat sparking in her belly. Pushing tentatively back against him, she gasped as a pleasurable bite of pain lanced through her belly.

"My Shadoe," he purred. She shrieked as his hand landed sharply on her ass — one, two, three times. "Your butt just turned the prettiest shade of pink. And I can smell your hot little pussy. You like being spanked, don't you?"

She whimpered, her head thrashing back and forth on the bed. "Benjamin, yes, hell, yes," she groaned.

Her breath froze in her lungs as she felt the head of his cock probing at the entrance to her ass. Thick, hot, harder than a length of iron, he pushed, his hands gripping her hips firmly as he forged deeper, unrelenting, until he was embedded completely inside of her. Shrieking, stuffed full, impaled on the hot length of his cock, she was caught between the pleasure and the pain.

He reached around and pinched her clit. She keened, a mini-orgasm tearing through her.

Bracing one hand low on her spine, he started to shaft her, slow and deep, as he whispered, "I love fucking your ass. You don't know whether you like it or not…even now. Even after you've come. I love watching this tight little hole opening for my cock, and I love listening to you whimper and moan as I drive inside you. You want it, even if you don't know if you like it or not…"

Shadoe screamed as he drove inside her with one particularly deep thrust, her body shuddering under the impact of it. She started to circle her fingers around her clit with quick hard strokes, her breath hitching in her lungs.

Deep inside her ass, he pushed, his cock searing hot, throbbing. He pulled out slowly, groaning as she pushed back instinctively, aching to keep him inside her.

He slapped her ass again and she sobbed.

The next thrust sent her soaring into climax, a dam breaking open inside her as she came and cream flooded from her cleft, soaking her busy fingers and his balls as they slapped against her.

"Hmmmm...perfect," he groaned. He threw back his head, and a long, eerie howl rose from his throat as he came, his cock jerking inside the snug glove of her ass as he pumped inside her, filling her with hot jets of sperm.

He sank down to rest against her quivering back as the milking sensations of her climax emptied him. His breath wheezed out of him and he asked weakly, "Are you ready to beg for mercy yet?"

"Uh-huh," she whimpered.

"Good. I think I need a nap now," he murmured. Easing them to the side, he slowly slipped out of her, shushing her softly as she flinched. And then they slid into sleep, their bodies spent.

* * * * *

Malachi alighted on the small strip of sidewalk, cocking his head. The hotel room was finally silent. "Dey are done... I tink," Leandra said from behind him, her voice wry.

He turned and met her eyes, not sure what he would find there.

When he saw acceptance, plain and simple, he didn't know what to think.

She smiled at him. Folding her arms around herself, she rubbed at them, feeling cold, and weaker than she had ever felt in her life. "I can't say dat I ever wanted to be a vampire," she told him, a smile canted that pretty mouth upwards. "But I've learned, over de past few months, mebbe I'm not an evil person. It's been driven home hard, over de past few weeks. I can live dis life. And it is a life… I'm thankful to have it. I didn't want to die. You saved me from dat."

Malachi stood, shocked as she moved up to him and rose to her toes, pressing her lips gently to his. "Thank you, Malachi."

Settling back on her heels, she studied him, a smile dancing around her lips. "You expected me t' hate ya, didn't ya?" she drawled, sounding more like her wry, sarcastic self.

"Aye," he said, simply. The burning in his eyes wasn't the sting of tears. He didn't know what it was. But it wasn't tears. He hadn't cried in…centuries, at least.

She grinned. "Well, if it would make ya feel better, I can always pretend for a while," she offered. "But I'd rather you offer to help me out wit dis new…vampire ting."

"Vampire thing?" he repeated, dismayed.

Her eyes sparkled. "Yes, vampire ting. Ya know, da feeding an' all. An' I don't plan on being a plain vampire," she teased. Her eyes glowed for the briefest second.

Malachi rolled his eyes skyward and whispered quietly, "Please help me."

So after centuries, he was finally roped into taking a student.

* * * * *

Shadoe studied the pile of stone in front of her.

Okay, so it wasn't a pile.

It was a rather elegant setting, this place Benjamin called Excelsior. But she didn't *want* to go to school.

Sliding him a narrow glance, she demanded, "Why can't you just teach me?"

"I'm not good enough," he said flatly, resting his hand on her neck.

The dominance of the gesture wasn't lost on her, and the wolf inside her sensed it, and shushed the part of her that would argue.

"I'm a decent witch. You are an exceptional one. I always knew I'd have to bring you here." His eyes closed and he licked his lips. "If I had brought you here from the first, maybe what happened could have been avoided."

A soft comforting presence surrounded them and the Wolf whispered into his mind, *Brother...then perhaps, the vampire Dumas would still be unknown to the Council. The witch Leandra and Malachi even now Hunt him. He will no longer prey on the world, unbeknownst to us. All things happen for a reason. All things.*

"He's right," Shadoe whispered, wrapping her arms around Ben and snuggling her cheek against his chest. "Besides, I doubt I would have listened to you at first."

He cocked a brow at her and asked, "Does that mean you're listening now?"

She smiled sunnily. "When it's in my best interest—of course."

"You're a brat, Shadoe, you know that?" he said levelly. But the pleasure, the laughter in her eyes made his heart dance. He doubted she would have been able to laugh even two months ago. He knew she hadn't ever had that kind of joy in her laughter.

Odd, how damn near losing her life a second time had given her that kind of freedom.

With a tug on her silky brunette curls, he led her down the path to Excelsior. "Come on. I've been promised a temporary teaching position...oh, the joy..."

Epilogue

Sheila glanced up as she sensed somebody new entering the school. She knew Cross—distantly.

Her eyes passed over him without much interest before they landed on the woman next to him. She smelled witch, she smelled shifter… A frown briefly marred her face before she turned back to the book she held.

It was a gory, bloody mystery.

And it wasn't holding her interest worth a damn.

She couldn't stop thinking of Rafe.

The bastard.

Those wicked black eyes, that clever mouth…she never should have slept with him.

That was her first big mistake.

The second was falling in love with him.

But she had done what she could to fix it. She had begged Eli to let her leave…he had agreed. To a vacation.

A vacation wasn't what she wanted but it was a start.

She wanted, desperately, to find some sunny beach, and some sexy surfer boy that she could use to forget Rafe. That is what she would have done, when she had been alive. Back in the eighties…all of twenty years ago.

What had she been thinking, falling in love with Rafe?

Closing her eyes, she turned her face to the wall and let the tears fall. She needed to get out of Excelsior and find a man. Have an affair—a hot, wild affair. No man could make her forget Rafe, but maybe she could get his smell off of her, and the memory of his touch would fade a little.

* * * * *

Rafe hadn't been able to find Sheila for three days. Not that he had been looking.

But when the sweet scent of plumeria started to fade from Eli's enclave, he knew something was going on.

Stalking into the Master's quarters with hell in his eyes probably wasn't the best way to start the day…but then again, for some odd reason, Rafe seemed to be spoiling for a fight all the time lately.

"Where's the little southern belle?" he demanded, flinging himself down onto a long leather couch.

Eli glanced up from his desk just in time to see the leather molding itself to the long, rangy vampire's form. And to see the fire in Rafe's gaze. He couldn't help the smile that filled his eyes, but he did manage to keep it from curling his lips.

"She's gone away for a while," he said, leaning back and folding his hands across his belly. "Sheila has been rather— unhappy," he mused after a moment. "She petitioned at first to leave, but we decided a vacation might suit."

"To leave?" Rafe growled.

"Yes. A new Master, she thought, a new home, might solve the problem she's been dealing with."

"What problem?" Rafe demanded, shooting to his feet. "She Hunts once a week, takes Erika shopping and acts like a babysitter for the kid. And cooking. Cooking, for crying out loud. What fucking problem?"

His black hair tumbled into his eyes and he shoved it aside as he started to pace, mumbling and swearing under his breath.

Eli heard every word.

"I believe she is lonely. I suggested she go find a man and get…fucked six different ways to Sunday. Well, that was Sarel's phrase. But it suits, I think," Eli said, bracing himself, and reminding himself staunchly that Rafe was a friend, and that killing him wouldn't help Rafe or Sheila's predicament.

Of course, when Rafe leaped over the desk and tore him out of his chair with startling speed, Eli did have to admit, he may have a bit of a fight on his hands. But he hadn't been planning on fighting at all. Throttling down the instinct to battle, he gave Rafe an innocent look and forced a fake bellow, "What the hell is your bloody problem?"

"You told her to what?" Rafe demanded in a low, deadly whisper.

"Fuck me, she's a lovely, loving young woman. And she's *lonely*. You don't want her anymore, but nobody here will give her a damn glance for fear of insulting you. She needs a man, so I told her to go *find* one," Eli said, reaching up and shoving Rafe back.

Rafe went flying, but he took a handful of Eli's silk vest with him. Glancing down, Eli scowled. "Now that was just uncalled for. Sarel bought that for me," he snapped as he took the tattered remains off and held it up. Even Sheila, with her talented hands couldn't fix this one. *If* she was around.

"You told her to go find a man," Rafe repeated, his fangs protruding past his upper lip, his black eyes gleaming red in his rage.

"Aye. I did." Eli allowed a tiny smile to appear as he cocked his head. "That really shouldn't be a problem for you...but it looks like it is. Why is that?"

Rafe went completely still as he glared at Eli.

And then he stalked out.

About the author:

They always say to tell a little about yourself! I was born in Kentucky and have been reading avidly since I was six. At twelve, I discovered how much fun it was to write when I took a book that didn't end the way it should have ended, and I rewrote it. I've been writing since then.

About me now... hmm... I've been married since I was 19 to my high school sweetheart and we live in the midwest. Recently I made the plunge and turned to writing full-time and am looking for a part-time job so I can devote more time to my family—two adorable children who are growing way too fast, and my husband who doesn't see enough of me...

Shiloh welcomes mail from readers. You can write to her c/o Ellora's Cave Publishing at 1056 Home Avenue, Akron OH 44310-3502.

Why an electronic book?

We live in the Information Age—an exciting time in the history of human civilization in which technology rules supreme and continues to progress in leaps and bounds every minute of every hour of every day. For a multitude of reasons, more and more avid literary fans are opting to purchase e-books instead of paperbacks. The question to those not yet initiated to the world of electronic reading is simply: *why?*

1. *Price.* An electronic title at Ellora's Cave Publishing and Cerridwen Press runs anywhere from 40-75% less than the cover price of the <u>exact same title</u> in paperback format. Why? Cold mathematics. It is less expensive to publish an e-book than it is to publish a paperback, so the savings are passed along to the consumer.

2. *Space.* Running out of room to house your paperback books? That is one worry you will never have with electronic novels. For a low one-time cost, you can purchase a handheld computer designed specifically for e-reading purposes. Many e-readers are larger than the average handheld, giving you plenty of screen room. Better yet, hundreds of titles can be stored within your new library—a single microchip. (Please note that Ellora's Cave and Cerridwen Press does not endorse any specific brands. You can check our website at www.ellorascave.com or

www.cerridwenpress.com for customer recommendations we make available to new consumers.)

3. *Mobility.* Because your new library now consists of only a microchip, your entire cache of books can be taken with you wherever you go.

4. *Personal preferences are accounted for.* Are the words you are currently reading too small? Too large? Too...**ANNOYING**? Paperback books cannot be modified according to personal preferences, but e-books can.

5. *Instant gratification.* Is it the middle of the night and all the bookstores are closed? Are you tired of waiting days—sometimes weeks—for online and offline bookstores to ship the novels you bought? Ellora's Cave Publishing sells instantaneous downloads 24 hours a day, 7 days a week, 365 days a year. Our e-book delivery system is 100% automated, meaning your order is filled as soon as you pay for it.

Those are a few of the top reasons why electronic novels are displacing paperbacks for many an avid reader. As always, Ellora's Cave and Cerridwen Press welcomes your questions and comments. We invite you to email us at service@ellorascave.com, service@cerridwenpress.com or write to us directly at: 1056 Home Ave. Akron OH 44310-3502.

COMING TO A BOOKSTORE NEAR YOU!

ELLORA'S CAVE

Bestselling Authors Tour

UPDATES AVAILABLE AT
WWW.ELLORASCAVE.COM

Discover for yourself why readers can't get enough of
the multiple award-winning publisher
Ellora's Cave.
Whether you prefer e-books or paperbacks, be sure to
visit EC on the web at www.ellorascave.com for an
erotic reading experience that will leave you
breathless.

www.ellorascave.com